North Morgan was born in 1980. I blog London Preppy, which has been featured in *Dazed & Confused*, *Time Out* and *Attitude* amongst other publications. London Preppy has been an international success, attracting over 1.5 million hits by the time North published his first short story as part of the *Boys & Girls* anthology, launched at the London Literature Festival in 2010. He published his debut novel *Exit Through The Wound* to critical acclaim in 2011 and *Highlights of My Last Regret* in 2014. *Love Notes to Men Who Don't Read* is his third novel.

He currently lives in California.

northmorgan.com

LOVE NOTES TO MEN WHO DON'T READ

NORTH MORGAN

LIMEHOUSE BOOKS

To Brett, John H, and Michael

INTRODUCTION

The world closed in on me, so I had to get out. On Saturday, having packed as much as I can into two large suitcases, I make my way to Heathrow Airport where I catch a flight heading west. Perhaps this is perceived to be an act of surrender, telling both of them that they won, though I've never been a combative person and this isn't a war. This, to me, is a way of figuring out what the hell happened, but in a different city, one where I don't feel this humiliated.

Following the events of the weekend of the 2nd / 3rd February, I break up with Brett. I stay in Berlin where I was visiting family for another week, as planned, and return to London, where we both live, on the 10th of February. I move my stuff out of our flat, and stay at a friend's place for a few weeks while I decide what I want to do.

During the three weeks that I'm in London, I find out that Brett and Frank are still seeing each other, going on dates, attending dinner parties as a couple. During these weeks, I also find out that Frank has a boyfriend that he lives with, who remains unaware of everything.

I contact the boyfriend and tell him what has been happening. The boyfriend refuses to believe me. I contact Brett and tell him about the boyfriend. Brett refuses to believe that the boyfriend exists. Brett contacts Frank and enquires about the boyfriend. Frank responds that there is a boyfriend but they've broken up. I message the boyfriend to confirm that they're still together, get a written response saying, "Yes, Frank and I are together", take a screenshot and forward it to Brett. A week later, I get a message from the boyfriend telling me that I was right and that he has now broken up with Frank. Two days after that, I find out that Brett and Frank are now officially boyfriends. Just to sum up: Me and the boyfriend out. Brett and Frank in.

Just to sum up further: On Wednesday 30th January, I say goodbye to my boyfriend of four years whom I live with and go to the airport

1

to fly back to Germany and visit my Mother. On Sunday 10ᵗʰ February I arrive back at the same airport, but my boyfriend now has a new boyfriend. Who also has another boyfriend. Someone I've hooked up with in the past before I met my boyfriend and he met his boyfriend.

This is who we are. This is my social group. We are gays living in big metropolitan areas heavily involved in the gay scene. We all know each other. We all have big muscles and violent abs and handsome faces and lots of disposable income and innumerable sexual partners, each one hotter than the next. We adopt variations of heteronormative looks (some of us are bros, some of us are jocks, some of us are simply worked-out guys next door), which we document incessantly on Facebook, Instagram and all your other surrounding news feeds and timelines. We will post pictures of us with our shirts off, standing together on party dancefloors or next to expensive hotel swimming pools, and sometimes we'll even quote *Mean Girls* and tag the picture with, "You can't sit with us." We go to the best parties, take the best drugs, and have VIP tickets for the best events. We don't even pay for them. Are you jealous of us?

In order to attract the right kind of attention, we will publicly maintain that this isn't who we really are. We don't want this. We'll say that we really want to settle down. We'll say that we want to start a family. We'll say that we find this kind of lifestyle empty, unfulfilling and horribly temporary. Who wants to be a messed up, single gay guy, going from gay bar to gay pride, we'll say, with nothing else of substance going on in his life? We will very carefully curate our public image to show how wholesome we are, and will balance out the pictures of our beautiful, half-naked friends, with pictures of our baby nephews (nieces much less popular) taken in bulk in the two hours every six months that we get to see them.

We fall in love with each other and we move in together, and retire from the scene for a few months, maybe a couple of years, because we have found happiness, and we don't need this any longer; we're over it. Then we fuck things up for fun or because we're bored, and we start going out again and seeing all the people we know – most of them are still there at a different stage of their own cycle – and we fall right back into place and we do it all over again.

We can have this forever. All that changes is that each time you go back there's one more person at the party that you have to avoid making eye contact with, or dancing too close to, because in the very recent past you destroyed their soul a little bit, or they destroyed yours.

MARCH 2013

1

My name is Konrad Platt and I have now been in America for eight days. This is a homecoming of sorts, as I was actually born here. My Father is American. My Mother is German. I only lived here for the first four years of my life and then moved to Berlin with Mum, after my parents' divorce, so we could be close to her family and she could get help bringing me up. Dad still lives in Pacific Palisades, California, where I am right now, and though we did see each other every couple of years when I was growing up, we've never been that close and he doesn't know much about what's happening in my personal life. He doesn't know that I'm gay, for one thing. It's not that he doesn't care, though I'm sure he does not, it's primarily that all this was a long time ago – it was 1984 when Mum and I moved to Europe – he's been re-married since, has had two more children with his second wife and I'm just part of a former life for him. About five years ago, I started working for him remotely from Europe (he owns an independent private wealth management firm) and even though our contact became much more frequent in professional terms, this never extended to our personal relationship.

When I was 16, I moved from Berlin to London, because it seemed exciting and because I wanted to. I went to college for my A-Levels there and then onto UCL where I studied Financial Risk Management. I worked for a couple different finance companies in London for a few years before taking the easy way out and going to work for Dad.

I came out in an uneventful way in my last year at university. It was London and nobody cared. My Mum and her family didn't care either. I did have some very predictable clichéd issues that tortured me for a few years before doing so, and I did spend some time viewing myself as a tragic figure, fighting internal battles, trying to overcome to perceived adversity of having had the terrible luck of being born a homosexual, but those are feelings everyone tends to have and if you manage to get over yourself pretty quickly, they won't even damage you too much.

So when I was in my second year at university I moved into a house share with three of my friends and we would all go out a lot and get drunk and all those guys would bring girls back home and sleep with them all the time, but I didn't do any of that, seeing that I had never had sex, and I think I might have kissed a total of three girls in my life but not for very long, and the idea was freaking me out. I thought I would never come out and I was planning to lead a pseudo-straight life, probably celibate, because being gay was too scary an option. Sometimes during that year, I would get on the tube in the evening by myself and sit there and go round in circles and think what I wanted to do with my life. Because London gives you lots of opportunities to do what you want and destroy your life a little bit, so I didn't want not to take advantage of those.

Other times, on a Saturday evening, when I had nothing to do, I would take the tube and go to Soho on my own and walk around a bit. And I would walk past gay shops and bars and bookstores, but I wouldn't walk in, because I was too embarrassed. Later that year, I would sometimes get the courage and I would go in and look at magazines and DVDs on the shelves, but I wouldn't pick them up, because I was scared I would draw attention to myself and somebody might see me from outside.

Around that time I decided that maybe I wanted to go ahead and meet a guy. I started going on an online dating site that is now defunct and I made a profile and put some pictures up, without showing my face. I was telling myself that I would meet somebody once, sleep with him, and then I would get this out of my system and be straight. I spent about four months talking to people on there and trying to find somebody that seemed like a decent person to do this with. I bought a laptop to go online with and I kept it hidden from my housemates. I kept it hidden behind a cupboard that I actually had to physically move to access, which was another self-imposed barrier to being gay. Like having to move a piece of furniture a few inches before accessing an online world of available men would be an actual barricade to acting on my sexuality.

One Friday in April, I met a guy. I didn't go to classes and I lied to my friends that I was going away for the day. I was meeting the guy at 11am and I was completely terrified, so I remember downing two beers and some vodka before I left home. I met him, we had coffee, I lied to him about my name, my age, where I'm from, what I did, everything. He was nice enough to pretend to believe me when I was telling him that I don't want to be gay, this would only be a one-off experience and I would never come out. We went back to his place and had sex.

I didn't tell anyone anything for another five months. The first person I told was Ben, my best friend from UCL. We were in some bar in Holborn after the summer break and the song that was playing was *Silver Screen Shower Scene* by Felix Da Housecat featuring Miss Kittin which has nothing to do with me coming out but I remember it very specifically and I told Ben I had something to say and I started crying because I thought he would never want to talk to me again and then I told him. It took another month until I told the second person and that was one of my other housemates. By the Christmas break of my third year at Uni, I had told all my friends in London and now it seems like a lifetime ago, if you are unfortunate enough for your lifetime to have only lasted twelve years.

I met Brett at an after club in North London over four years ago. He was interesting, handsome, and he was a born and bred Londoner, which was very important to me at the time because I wanted to have roots in this city. At the same time, I wasn't really looking for a relationship. I had broken up with my first boyfriend, George, six months before. George and I had been together for a few years and eventually realised we were now just friends, so we transitioned into that. I was quite content with my love life – there were enough people in London to fuck, mess around with, lead on and get led on by, but I don't suppose you can choose when these things will happen. Brett had had a more dramatic break up just a few weeks before meeting me. He was looking around more actively than I was, probably trying to meet somebody else and get over the ex. We slept together the first night, of course, but then uncharacteristically kept seeing each other. We became boyfriends a few weeks later. The following year, we moved in together. In the four years that we were together, at first we went out a lot. Then we stayed in a lot. We traveled together. I spent time with his family. He flew to Berlin with me often to visit my Mum. We were monogamous. We got bored of monogamy and had threesomes. We felt bad about having threesomes and became monogamous again. We fought and broke up and got back together again and we got a puppy together. We talked about getting married. We were typically gay. During the last year of the relationship things had changed a little bit. There was a general sense that perhaps Brett didn't love me as much as I loved him. It felt like he was losing interest. But it's easier to recognise that now, in retrospect, knowing exactly how things ended. At the time, I guess I didn't really want to see it.

In the eight days that I've lived in my Dad's house in the Palisades, I haven't actually left the pool house where I'm staying once. I'm having a wonderful time sobbing, staring blankly into space in what I believe is a hugely dramatic way, not listening to sad break-up music because I'm too upset even to do that, researching methods of a painless suicide (there are none, nothing is as effortless as you want it to be unless you have a gun and even that's not guaranteed to put you out of your misery) and watching every move that Brett and his new boyfriend are making online, and they're making many moves because they're very proud and want to show each other off, and avoiding to eat. My Dad and his wife, who hardly know me that well anyway and don't know the reasons why I decided to pick up and move across the world and into their place all of a sudden must think that I'm completely insane.

2

Last Sunday, I moved to West Hollywood. I only know one person who lives in LA apart from my Dad and his family, a kid called Anthony who's 24, from London and moved here a couple of months ago. Well, I know a few people from the gay scene because I've met them at parties around the world, but Anthony is the only one that I've spent any time one-on-one with and have lived in the same city as, before. Anthony is quite short, maybe around 5'9", unnaturally muscular, with a marine haircut and covered in badass tattoos. I realise I just described everyone who has stepped foot in a gay bar in the western hemisphere in the last five years. From what I understand Anthony left London to come check out LA because he was bored, and now he's moved in here with a rich stoner guy called Markus, who's funding his lifestyle and their mutual drug habit. In his spare time from doing nothing at all, Anthony dances on a 40" x 40" podium in a bar on Santa Monica Boulevard.

When Anthony found out that I'm here now and the details of my break up, he insisted that the only way I'm going to feel better is if I put an end to my self-imposed isolation at my Dad's pool house and move to WeHo to meet some new people and start moving on. My emotional state is such right now that I'll happily take serious life advice from an aimless go-go dancer, so I found a one-bedroom apartment, picked up my bags, and moved.

On this Friday, I finish work and I drive to the gym like I have done every day this week. In the lift on the way up to the gym from the parking garage there are two bros in gym clothes and an old lady, who must be going to the Whole Foods next to the gym.

She looks up at them wearing full douchebag attire, including sweatbands around their heads, and says:

"Are you boys going to the gym?"

The one gym bro who's hotter and looks like more of a dick smirks and says, "Yeah".

Then old lady continues:

"To exercise and get buff?"

He laughs and says "yeah" again.

"And get those six-packs abs?"

Then the gym bro lifts his shirt up and says, "I already have those", and I want both to kill him and jerk off on his stomach. Then the lift gets to the gym floor and we all get out.

Today I'm working out my shoulders. In the gym, there's a boy whom I've seen every time I've come here, always in the evening, always with a friend of his (invisible) and the thing about this boy, who cannot be any older than 19, maybe 20, is that he's tall and blond, and has a toned body, fine, but he also has a pair of blue eyes that have that effect on me where if they catch mine, my heart stops for a moment and I have to take a second to remember a) where I am and b) what I am doing. This is not an effect to be taken lightly and it takes a very particular shade of blue for it to happen. The fact that his eyes look like they've witnessed an impossible tragedy, quite possibly some genocide, and will never recover only adds to it. So because this feeling that I get when I look at him in the eyes is very, very disturbing, but also very exhilarating, I can't help but seek it out. And I keep staring at him. Because I keep staring at him, he tends to look back, and to cut a long story short, when this boy is in the gym, nothing really gets done. Not that I want anything from this boy, other than to occasionally get the electric shock he seems to be able to readily inflict on my nervous system.

Now, apart from my own personal fetish for arctic blue eyes that reflect centuries of endless sorrow, this boy is also overwhelmingly good looking objectively. And I stand there and look at him and keep thinking of the time when it will all come together in four or five years from now and he's turned into an actual god, and how he will deal with his life then, a life where everyone around him will be falling over themselves to make things easy for him and get close to him and take advantage of him, generally a life in the bubble that those extraordinarily good looking people live in and the rest of us will never experience.

Then I go back home, and it's Friday evening and Anthony comes over with Markus and they want to go out, but I don't feel like it so I ask them to go if they like, but I'll stay in and watch some TV and then go to bed. Then Anthony and Markus go out. I start watching the first movie that shows up as I'm flicking through the channels. This movie stars some big-name white American actors and a number of unknown Indian actors and appears to be all about prejudice, integration, cultural assimilation and the surprising enormity of the human spirit, but I'm not really paying any attention. Instead I keep thinking of Brett in London and missing him and reminiscing about all our time together and wondering what we would be doing on this Friday night if we were still together like we were two months ago and trying to guess what he's doing right now with someone else instead, so eventually I turn off the TV and make a half-assed attempt at meditating and clearing my head because someone advised me to do that, but I don't really know how to meditate so this results in me staring blankly at the wall for the next two hours or so, and then I fall asleep.

3

On my first Saturday in LA I go out to meet some friends for one of those friends' birthday, and I'm using the term friends perhaps in a delusional way, because I don't really know anyone in LA.

These are Anthony's friends. I don't know that LA is filled with people who want to be my friends anyway; I think I'm too intense and gloomy even in my most upbeat moments, and nobody has time for that here. Here, even in just one week I've met people who tell me that they're writers and they love Kafka, but in subsequent conversation I discover that they've never blacked out or fallen in a k hole in their lives, I mean how is that even possible, or people who read the cover of the book I'm holding back to me and pronounce Proust, 'Praust', as in Faust. There's nothing wrong with not liking Kafka, of course, and not knowing how to pronounce Proust, but please stop pretending.

We end up at some boring old warehouse party in downtown LA and nobody in my group pretends that this was a smart choice, but some of them become more easily accustomed than others because they're better at finding pills and one of those friends who is very good at finding pills comes up to me at some point for an intimate bonding moment and tells me something along the lines of: welcome to LA, I hope you don't get sucked into the gay scene here, just be careful.

And I find that upsetting, because, well, how do you tell somebody that his warning has arrived too late? How do you tell him you were sucked in several years ago and are still trying to find a way out? When I came out at 20 and started going to these places I used to think I'd never be doing this at 30. I'm 33 and, still, here I am. But as you get older, your self-imposed timeline keeps getting extended. Right now, can I really set my gay scene getaway at 35 with any sort of conviction? What about 40? Can I genuinely promise to myself that I won't be 42 and crawling around some gay party with my shirt off?

Unfortunately some gay men never grow old. Gay men like me. Out of all those gays in the suburbs, leading the dreary lives that I so want, maybe some used to go out. Maybe some had been sucked in and they managed to escape. But I think that most of them never got involved in the first place. Not to the extent that I have and the people around me have. And those people from the suburbs won't touch me or the likes of me. The likes of me will continue to live in central London, LA, New York, etc, and find ourselves in infernal clubs on Saturday nights at 4am, passing around delayed warnings about avoiding to get sucked in.

APRIL 2013

4

The one good thing that is happening specifically in LA and more generally in my life right now, is that I have finally figured out the training schedule of the hot straight guys in my gym. And now I can shift my life around that and "accidentally" turn up at the same time. There is a group of around six or eight of them and they may not all be there consistently working out together always, but if you go between the hours of 8.30pm and 10.30pm on any given night, you will find at least three or four. This is a bit late in the day and it intervenes with one's dinner plans and sleeping needs, but luckily I have neither of those, so I'm there.

Like any social clique, this one has its own rules, behavioural modes and hierarchies. Some of the bros are more outgoing. Some are quieter. Some are more submissive. And there is one clear leader. Despite their individual roles and idiosyncrasies, there are two stable factors that apply to the group as a whole: a) they only talk to each other and dismiss everyone else in the gym, and b) there is not a single one of them I would not fuck.

My love affair with the group started in the locker room toilets, although unfortunately this is not as crude as it first sounds. You can tell a lot about a man's sexuality and place in the world by the way he behaves in a public toilet. As an incurable homosexual with confidence issues, taking a piss at a urinal is already a huge challenge for me. I'll always choose the cubicle if there is one, but if not, I will go for the urinal that's as far away as possible and I will stand there for minutes trying to force myself to go, playing various mental games as a distraction, whilst at the same time praying that nobody else shows up next to me. If someone does and he's straight, eight out of ten times he will arrive, get his dick out, start pissing like it's fucking nothing, finish, shake it off, slap it back in and walk away all in the same time that I've been standing there next to him holding mine and counting the tiles in front of me in the faint hope that *something* will start streaming out of it as I slowly die of embarrassment. Because, you know…he knows what's happening. He can hear the silence.

Two weeks ago, when some meathead I was seeing for the first time stood at the urinal next to me and started peeing using one hand only while employing the other one to pick sunflower seeds out of his basketball shorts' pocket and transfer them into his mouth where he cracked the shells open before spitting them out, I knew that I had no chance. I was in love. Imagine the confidence of being able to pee at the urinal uninterrupted as if no one else is around, but please, take a minute and imagine the confidence of doing this very thing while also eating. This person was some sort of god. The fact that this endeavour may have been kinda filthy and very inconsiderate (think of the poor cleaner having to pick the sunflower seed shells out of the urinal) but since when have bad manners and insolence been detrimental to carnal attraction? He could have brought in a trashcan and emptied it there for all I care. I probably would have liked him more.

After that incident, I followed the guy to the gym floor. He led me to my now beloved group of douchebag straight bros, and I haven't looked back since.

On this Wednesday evening, this guy, the leader, is there with three of his subordinates, plus the addition of blonde girl, who seems to be his girlfriend. She is Christina Aguilera straight out of the *Dirrty* video. I know that's from fifteen years ago, but in certain parts of Southern California it's considered a classic, timeless look. As part of a plan to attract all the attention he can possibly get (even though him just existing there immobilised in a tank filled with formaldehyde like Damien Hirst's shark would be more than enough for me to stand and stare for at least two months) the leading gym meathead is performing an impossible, completely useless, and highly dangerous task with a 45lbs barbell.

He is lying on the floor flat on his back. Next to him is the barbell with added 45lbs weight plates on each side. With one hand, he grabs the bar in the middle and slowly sits up, then eventually stands up with his arm extended up over his head holding the 135lbs weight in perfect balance. One of the subordinates and his girlfriend are filming this on their phones. All three of the men watching are shouting encouraging comments, like, "Yeah buddy!" and "Get it, boy". When this is done, they all cheer. The leader puts the weight on the floor and kneels down to allow his girlfriend to climb on his shoulders. He lifts her up and they both flex their biceps, while two of the subordinate males take more pictures.

When I go home later in the evening, even before stalking Brett and his new boyfriend online, I open Instagram and search by the gym geotag. Sure enough, I find two posts: the video of the weight lift has been posted by one of the other bros and the picture with the girlfriend on the shoulders has been posted by the girlfriend. The meathead that I like is tagged in both. I check his profile but there isn't much on there. I then check the girlfriend's. She has over five hundred posts and every single one of them includes the hashtag #savedbyLA. She has many pictures with her gym boyfriend, in several of which he is shirtless (they seem to like the beach) even though the relationship appears to be only three-four weeks old. In her latest post, the one of her sitting on his shoulders, she has commented, "His love roared louder than her demons." I don't understand any of it. How was this Christina Aguilera lookalike saved by LA? What were her demons? I have demons. Where is my gym meathead? Who's going to save me? I follow both of them in pursuit of answers and go to bed.

5

On Wednesday morning I wake up. I am very unhappy. It was a really smart idea to run away from London and try to get over my heartbreak in a whole new city where I don't know anyone. Seeing that I don't have anyone to talk to in real life, I go online. After my usual check in with Brett's social media so that I get that daily stab in the heart, I start wasting time reading about music.

I spend a lot of time on an online messageboard called Popjustice where hundreds of people discuss and analyse pop stars and pop music relentlessly with forensic attention to detail and almost terrifying dedication. All those hundreds of people are gay and the music that they like is primary big commercial pop, like Lady Gaga and Rihanna and Britney Spears. Sometimes male pop stars too, and sometimes more obscure pop, but mainly pop fronted by all singing, all dancing powerful females. Those guys live for this type of music. They listen to it, watch it, then go on the Internet and spend hours talking about it. They even use a very specific vernacular to talk about pop music and to each other, a lot of which is borrowed from ball culture, as seen in the *Paris Is Burning* documentary, and has more recently been widely popularised amongst gay men by *Ru Paul's Drag Race* and the internet overall. On the Popjustice messageboard, there is always a young gay guy whose wig has been snatched by a new pop video that just dropped, and there's always a young gay guy who is spilling the tea on a pop album that's about to leak. I have absolutely no interest in listening to the music that these people talk about, and I don't necessarily think that it's because my internalised homophobia extends that far. I just like alternative music, mainly, and have done so since I was thirteen years old and discovering The Smiths, New Order, Suede, and other bands like that. However, this is literally the most visited website on my internet browser outside social media and porn. And despite not caring at all about the music they discuss, I care very much about the way that they do it and the things that they say. I love it so much when Beyoncé appears on a red carpet somewhere and a thousand twinks go online and declare that she's giving them life. I love it so much when Christina Aguilera does a live performance and murders a note and half of the posters are slain by her anyway and the other half tear her apart. A lot of the time, most of the time, I don't even listen to the songs or watch the performances they talk about, but I just log on and read their overdramatic hyper-gay reactions and I find that extremely satisfying. I guess that no matter how masculine I want to appear on the outside and how turned on I become by any moronic pseudo-bro with steroid muscles and a backward baseball cap, deep inside me there is a very girly, very repressed fag that is dying to find someone to relate to. So I read and I read and I read about Kylie Minogue's Christmas album and Britney Spears' Las Vegas residency and the pre-chorus to Arianna Grande album tracks that I'll never hear and it warms my broken gay little heart.

6

On this Friday, my friend William comes to visit from London on his way to Australia. We are all very international gays, you see, and we can't settle for one country. Even limiting yourself to one continent is just laughable; circuit parties happen just about everywhere.

William's visiting and staying at my place in LA, and while I'm pushing for a nice weekend catching up on some *Frasier*, maybe a stroll down to the local park, William has big going out plans and cannot be contained. I mean, I've always been kinda boring and a bit of a difficult person to get on with, but now because I'm heartbroken and have unjustly chosen to blame the gay scene for everything that happened to me, my internalised homophobia has kicked into high gear and I must be truly insufferable to hang out with.

William has two modes: either studying hard for some upcoming medical exam, during which time he won't pick up the phone to see how you are (that's irony for you) or, when the exam is over, party party party. These days I have two modes also: watching *Frasier*, or being dragged out and ruining everyone else's good time by insisting we go back. Thankfully for William, everyone else we know in LA has one mode only and that is party party party party. That's one more "party" than William. These words are not typed at random.

On Saturday evening, William, Anthony and I go and meet another LA-based friend of William's called Scott. Scott lives up in the Hollywood Hills and has a fantastic view of the city, so we just stay inside and get stoned. While I waste my high tying and untying my Sperry shoelaces over and over again, one of the others comes up with the idea that we should go to Palm Springs. It doesn't matter that it's nearly midnight on the Saturday; these people are still making plans for going away this weekend. Things move pretty quickly and then next morning we find ourselves driving down to Palm Springs.

We check in to the Ace hotel and spend the day by the pool. Apparently the Ace hotel used to be a thing, but people have moved on now and the crowd is not remotely gay or sceney enough. We are all extremely disappointed, but we proceed to get very drunk and that helps things quite a lot.

In the evening we go over to somebody's house party, where the main event is a huge outdoor screen by the swimming pool playing the film *Showgirls*. Because, you know, it's trashy. We gays love trashy things, but most of all trashy celebrities. Lindsay Lohan, right? Isn't she such a mess? I mean, she has a drug addiction and is throwing her life away. We'd never do that. We've got our lives together. Let's ironically worship Lindsay instead. The highlight of this house party, culturally, is when two gays jump in the swimming pool and recreate the bad sex scene between Elizabeth Berkley and Kyle MacLachlan from the film (lots of screaming, writhing, splashing around) as it plays on the big screen. A lot of people are filming or taking pictures of this on their phones, and when it's done, everyone erupts into wild applause.

MAY 2013

7

The most difficult thing about being gay in this time and age is figuring out a way to integrate into a primarily straight society that has now started to accept you. In the past things were a lot clearer. You just had to hide. Now that you don't have to do that anymore, how are you supposed to behave? It seems that the answer for a large part of the gay population is still the same: you must try to fit in. Heteronormativity is such a dirty little job, but a lot of people choose to do it. You have to appear to be masculine. You have to appear to reject promiscuity. And now that it is an option for you finally, you really have to appear to aspire towards a traditional family model, like the one you were brought up in (ludicrously high divorce rates everywhere in the western world notwithstanding).

Because this is currently a very popular look, mentions of wanting a family and how many children you would like to have are now very common flirting techniques. Because, you know, this is a way to show that you're not like those gays, the gays who were previously conspicuous within the overall social consciousness: selfish, lewd, hedonistic, and shortsighted. Instead, you are someone with substance and strong morals. Modern gays love a strong foundation. At the same time, the fast-paced, hook up gay culture is nowhere near letting up. I don't know how much casual sex gay men had in the 70s, 80s and 90s, but I'm willing to guess that it's no more than what people have now with access to all these bars, clubs, and hook up apps.

So it's a bit of a conundrum. Who are you supposed to be when culture moves one way, a way that assimilates you to a heteronormative society, but behaviourally you're not there and may never be?

These social factors do vary a lot, of course, depending on where you live even within those western countries that are becoming much more accepting. In America, even though the official line at a top national level is one of gay acceptance and equal rights support, there is huge variation on a regional level. Suburban Nashville is not the same as downtown Manhattan. But I think that the South drives the country's gay identity as much as NYC does just by the sheer volume of the population that lives there.

Religion does play a huge role and America is still a very religious place any way you look at it. It is much more religious than either of the two other countries I have lived in, Germany and the UK. When I was growing up in Germany, the church had absolutely no relevance in my life. My maternal grandparents already didn't go to church. In the east almost everyone is atheist. In the south and south west where they're Catholic, people tend to be a little more religious though young people do not generally go to church.

In America, and particularly in the South where the regional identity and pride seem to be stronger than anywhere else, you are very likely to find gay men in their 20s and 30s who are fervently Christian. I have seen Instagram accounts of gay men who live in the South, whose descriptive tagline has been, "God. Country. Family." In Germany the dictum "Für Gott und Vaterland" ("For God and fatherland") exists, but I don't think the average gay man my age or younger strongly associates with it. So morality and behavioural expectations are very complicated for gay men right now, and possibly more complicated for gay men in America compared to the more liberal European countries in the north there. And perhaps it would be easier not to think about these things at all, but I'm here now and have nothing else to distract myself with, so I do.

8

On Wednesday I start my day with my part-time occupation of scrolling through Instagram and looking at hot guys that I never want to have anything to do with in real life because they seem like cunts, plus they would never talk to me anyway.

My first discovery of the day is a guy called Shawn, who lives in Boston. Shawn is thick as fuck and has a shaved head and a blond fuzzy beard. His face is practically square and just by looking at him I really want him to head-butt me and leave me bleeding on the ground outside an Irish pub in the city centre of Boston, after I mistakenly touched his hand while ordering a beer at the crowded bar, which he took as a sign that I'm some fag hitting on him.

Shawn appears to be spending his time uploading videos on Instagram of him performing Crossfit exercises without a shirt on and adding commentary like, "Getting my jump rope skills ready for the @Crossfit metcon. Can't wait to PR this weekend on my lifts #liftoff #crossfitgames #liftheavy #nobelt #epicresults" and "305# x 2 Push Press". I can't decipher this highly advanced code, but it's really turning me on whatever the hell it means. He also seems to make a living by selling personalised workouts and diet programmes to his 45.4k followers, all of which I can get for free on any random bodybuilding messageboard after spending two seconds online. But somehow, somewhere stupid people exist that prefer to send their money to Shawn and get them from him.

I review Shawn's profile and admire how much of an asshole and how straight he is, but the further I go deeper into his 695 posts that date back three years ago, the more suspicious I get. The Crossfit doesn't start until a 65 weeks ago, the beard doesn't appear until 97. Long before the videos of him mouthing "Bitch you guessed it, hoo, you woz right" to some rap song playing while he's doing squats in the gym, I find a video of him singing along to something that sounds to me conspicuously like a musical number with his own voice…and he sounds good. Bros don't ad lib to *Defying Gravity* from *Wicked*.

So I take this investigation to Google and start searching his name. And I am devastated to find that Shawn, before the steroids and facial hair, was a minor Broadway actor. I am even more devastated to find that he was pretty much openly gay, until the musical career disintegrated and the times changed, of course, and he had to move back to Boston from NYC and reinvent himself as an aggressively heterosexual online personal trainer.

Just before my attraction to him disappears completely, I am blessed by some sort of divine inspiration and type his name into Google followed by the word "naked". Ten minutes later I have downloaded and jerked off to two videos of him that someone has saved from the time when Shawn was selling live webcam shows, presumably to fund himself between his two careers. I unfollow him on Instagram, because there's nothing to put you off a straight bro faster than seeing him type, "Tip me", when the webcam show client has asked him to bend over and finger himself (which he does), but I actually save the videos to watch again in the future, because I'm a hypocrite and the attraction hasn't gone at all, I just don't want to encourage his fake bro transformation by following him on social media.

9

Almost three months into living in the U.S., I am starting to understand what's up. At some point in the last five years, "bro", the movement in which affirming your masculinity means emulating the appearance and behaviour of 22-year-old frat boys, overtook "urban" as the predominant aspirational youth culture in America. I don't know why it happened. It happened. I remember when everyone was trying to be all gangsta when I was living in London in my late 20s. Well, now everyone wants to be just a chill bro. Chillen the eff out. Chillen the eff out at Coachella, sports games, maybe the old tailgate. With Bud Light.

These cultural trends don't bypass the gays, of course. We're all still fucking broken and want to belong. We'll latch on to whatever heteronormative fad comes along. Bring them on. In fact, we won't just latch on. We'll take them on, give them a few spins, mix them up with our personal struggle and psychodrama, and throw them back in your face in caricature form. I remember all the gays who turned up in the clubs with the big gold chains, giant hi-tops and elaborate trucker hats. Well as the equivalent of the urban gay, we now get the gay bro.

I was fortunate enough that the whole urban phenomenon passed me by. I didn't get it. I wasn't attracted to it. I used to see those kids, who were really, really popular, by the way, and think – well, what difference does it make if you're wearing a thick gold chain around your neck and have a smoking gun tattooed on you? You're an insecure gay guy, no different to me, and you're fronting like crazy. It's a Halloween costume.

I am unfortunate enough, though, that the whole gay bro phenomenon doesn't pass me by at all. I see them, and I want them. I fall for their Halloween costume. I want to sleep with it. The word that I use is "unfortunate", because the people who tend to take these strong, masculine identities and adopt them full-time and live them day after day and actually believe them, tend to be the people who are most insecure about their sexuality. This covert unavailability does not stop the attraction. There is such a thing as emotional masochism, after all.

No good is going to come from pursuing a relationship with a gay bro. A full-time masc musc gay bro, who's convinced himself that he's not a "typical gay", is a walking vision of internalised homophobia. Do you think a gay bro is ready to hold you in his big arms, lie in bed with you at night, look into your eyes and tell you that he loves you? I do not. I think the full-time, masc musc gay bro has to learn to love himself first.

Now, the fact that I've typed out the last two paragraphs is ridiculous in itself, I know. I might as well be reading them out loud to myself in the mirror. In the three months that I've lived in America, despite all my cheerlessness and self-imposed isolation, I have found the time to become obsessed with the bro phenomenon and attempted to take it on myself. Yeah, I can say that I'm self-aware and I'm subverting it and even mocking it, but in reality perhaps I am just perpetuating it, perhaps I do hate myself as much as I claim that those people do.

Anyway, this is not about me. This is about bros. How do you find them? How do you identify them in the street, on the beach, in the gay bar where a friend dragged them, honestly, they'd rather be at a sports bar drinken Bud Light, how do you take them home and have emotionless, guilty-yet-passionate sex with them before they pass out next to you with their arm squashing your chest while you lie awake on your back staring at the ceiling? (Bros don't lose any sleep).

Being a bro is an all-encompassing endeavour that requires concentrated efforts combining different aspects like their mentality, their behaviour, and their look.

First of all mentally, they kinda have to play a little dumb. Bros may come with a wide range of intelligence, but the smarter ones can't let you know that. No one is going to take a bro seriously if he exhibits a high level of intellect. It just takes away from his swag. Of course, bros are not allowed to read anything, so throw away your books. Books just turn them off. A very quick way to come across as a moron is to misspell everything. Key words to spell wrong are the present participle forms of every verb. For example: they can never type "just chilling". It always has to be "just chillen". "Drinking" is "drinken", "golfing" is "golfen", etc. Spelling things wrong adds to the perceived insolence that's a key aspect of the bro persona. Of course the bro doesn't care about you. He doesn't even care enough to use the autocorrect suggestion. You can take it or leave it. (I'll take it). No one can ever convince me that when I receive a text message that describes something as "amaxing", the bro did this by accident. Or that his iPhone didn't suggest "amazing" instead. It's just that the bro chose it this way, as part of his act. Sometimes he will also text you with ridiculous typos, which again, should not be happening in the day and age of autocorrect, but here we are and they do. When you receive a text that includes the words "maYbe" or "headingt to th game", you know that he ignored the autocorrect suggestion. The message the bro is sending you is that he doesn't have the time for this shit. He's heading to the game. You'll figure it out.

Bros have a very particular way of speaking to each other, as well as other people. All communication should start with "sup" or "whaddup" and everyone should be addressed with "bro", "bruh", "brah" (both are acceptable), "boss", "dawg", or even the classic, "dude". They can call their gym buddies "dude", but they can also call their Mother "dude". It's one and the same.

In terms of interests, everything falls under three categories: sports, drinking, and shitty music.

Sports, in particular, is what they were put on this planet to do. They were put on this planet to play sports and they were put on this planet to follow sports. But they have to make sure everyone around knows about it, because that is the most important part. They can be hapless and incompetent at physical activity, but they have to talk about it a lot anyway with the confidence of a state champion. A strong connection with "the outdoors" is also essential. Bros pretend like they have a horrible aversion to staying indoors. They pretend like their spirit cannot be contained within four walls. They pretend like they're always on their way to some badass outdoor activity. Only last week I was talking to some dude on Grindr and he told me that he got a job offer in Seattle, but he was never going to leave Southern California, because "he practically lives outside". I knew right then that he had just taken a piece of my heart. I knew right then that I would be spending several sleepless nights thinking about him. Then he blocked me.

Bros drink. A lot. Watery American beer, mainly, but also bourbon, shots, and wine when they want to be more sophisticated at a dinner party (before asking the host if there's any beer, actually, or failing that, bourbon). If they're tailgating, which combines their two main raisons d'etre – sports and drinking – they'll basically drink anything and everything that will get them the most paralytic, the quickest.

Music choices include EDM and country. That's it. Bros have to attend Coachella, of course, which is unofficially known as Heteronormative Christmas, but they don't have to watch any of the faggy alternative bands. They can just spend three days in Sahara, the DJ tent, where they will drink, hook up, intimidate other festival goers, and perform the trademark bro dance of extending their right arm high above their head with an open palm facing down and moving it to the beat while they're standing still. Oh, they may also jump up and down briefly when their pills kick in. They also tend to attend Stagecoach, obviously. Stagecoach is a country music festival that takes place in the same venue as Coachella, a week later, and it single-handedly stands for everything I both despise and lust over when it comes to American bros.

When they're having their picture taken, the primary goal is to come across as a badass. It is imperative that they do one of following: a) stick their tongue out in a silly / insolent way (the right expression comes with time and practice), b) wink, and c) give the camera the finger. I've never seen a bro do all three together and I think it may be possible in Florida, exclusively.

Finally, the look. Bros' whole look is pretending not to have one. They're not like the other gays who worry about clothes, fashion, looks, and trends. They're too straight actin for that. Bros wear what makes them feel comfortabol. This is, naturally, bullshit. Bros care about their look *a lot*. There is no other scientific explanation as to why all of them, bro after bro, make the same clothing / accessory choices. There is no other reason why they rest their sunglasses on the back of their neck, instead of the top of their head. It's impractical and they might lose them. But they still do it, because at some point they saw another bro wearing them that way, and this bro didn't look like he cared about his sunglasses, so now neither do they.

Other key fashion choices are: bandanas, lanyards to carry their keys, anything with a USA flag print, hoodies, socks pulled up high at the gym, wearing their t-shirt inside out because they happened to put it on that way and don't care enough to change it, anything from Under Armour, those compression shorts that you wear underneath your shorts at the gym / when you play sport, boat shoes with board shorts, boat shoes with white socks, Nike, flannel shirts when they're in a gay club because they don't need to show off their muscles, and the ultimate bro accessory – the backward baseball cap.

The backward baseball cap is the one, conclusive, unquestionable statement to the world that this bro may be gay, but he's also masc musc non-scene. These people are not taken seriously as a bros, unless they wear a backward hat at least 80% of the time. For the other 20%, they turn it forwards. The choice of baseball caps that they make is very wide. They do find it safer to stick to the classics though: their college team, their hometown team, the team of a city they've never been to but like the colours of, any fucking team will do. They can mix it up with some Nike or Under Armour, occasionally. They don't wear one of those big caps with the gay slogans though, as their backward baseball cap must never be humourous or camp. Those caps are exactly the opposite of what they're trying to do. Bros wear their baseball cap everywhere. There are literally no fucking limits. They can wear it in the gym and sweat through it like a motherfucker (but they'll look masculine), they can wear it to the gay bars (and they'll look non-scene and everyone will want to fuck them) and they can even wear it in the evening at semi-formal dinners with a long-sleeved, button down shirt (and they'll look fratty, which is something they want).

That's it. It's quite easy for most people to follow these rules and become a bro. If someone does, I will probably want him. If someone already knows me and I don't currently want him, he can try putting on a backward baseball cap. I will probably change my mind immediately and suddenly want him. And this is a very serious problem.

JUNE 2013

10

Heartbreak is really funny to anyone who's not suffering it. It comes with all sorts of overreaction and volatile behaviour. Imagine the heartbreak caused by your partner leaving you for someone else. You will feel bitter, you will feel wronged, and you will most likely feel quite vengeful. That's bound to cause you to be a little irrational. You'll want everyone to know what happened to you and that it wasn't your fault. And if you're not the person who's feeling this way, if you're just an outsider observing, this will all be quite hilarious. Do I think that for the end of any relationship only one person is to blame? I don't. And was I completely surprised when Brett walked out on me after four years together and started dating someone else without even flinching? Was I under the impression that everything was going so perfectly between us and when it ended the way it did, was I completely blindsided? Again, no. But being aware of these things is not making this any easier.

Being in LA is also not making this any easier. I'm surrounded by people that I don't know very well and although I tried their approach, to go out in full force and start living my life again, I'm just not ready. I need to be near people that I know a little better and I need to take a step back. The only friend in this whole continent that I've known for a long time and is completely outside this circle is my friend Willa who went to Uni in London, where we met, before moving back to the U.S. a few years later. She lives in San Francisco with her husband. They've offered to put me up for as long as I need to figure out what I want to do next. In the first weekend of June, I pack the few things that I have again, leave my short-let apartment in WeHo, and drive north.

There's nothing to say about the first couple of weeks. I don't eat, I don't sleep, I don't work, I don't listen to music or watch TV or read. I just wait. I also don't want to have anything to do with any guy who goes out and is part of the gay scene because, possibly as some sort of coping mechanism inspired by my own gay insecurities and self-loathing, I'm putting a lot of the blame for what happened on this. The gay lifestyle: going out, sleeping around, getting drunk, taking drugs, the bars and clubs and parties. Like non-scene gays or even straight people have never been cheated on and dumped before. So I guess I'm happily entertaining my delusions that I will eventually find contentment if I stay isolated in this house shared with my straight friends long enough.

Apart from being inactive and waiting, I continue to seek out updates of what's going on in London with Brett and his new boyfriend. This is extremely self-destructive, of course, but it's not something I can stop myself from doing. And the more I find out, the crazier I get.

How is it possible that someone can have a boyfriend for four years (very publicly, of course, with everyone in their circle knowing about it, as would be the case half a decade later) then suddenly, they turn up at a party or someone's birthday or wherever one week later, with a new man on their arm and nobody questions this? That's one of my thoughts. And I ask that question to my friend Sean in London, who's very bitter and homophobic himself, I guess, and Sean says:

"Because we're gay. This is expected. This is a culture where you're at a dinner party, then three people disappear from the table and the next thing you know is that they're all fucking in the bathroom. You think that anyone will raise an eyebrow at some London queen changing boyfriends all of a sudden?"

And I don't want him to have a point, but I don't know that he does not.

On Wednesday I'm chatting on Facebook with my friend Todd and Todd is American but lives in Australia, which is very convenient for me, as it gives me somebody to talk to when America has gone to bed and Europe hasn't woken up yet. It may be useful to add at this point that I have currently run out of sleeping pills. After Australia I start talking to Central Europe, after that Western Europe, after that the East Coast of America, and by the time I catch up with my own time zone on the West Coast I haven't slept for three days, but at least I have been very social.

Todd has a bad history of being attracted to terrible, terrible people who treat him like shit, but he just can't help it. He wants it really bad. These terrible, terrible people exhibit all sorts of objectionable behaviour, like cheating on him behind his back, being hookers behind his back, being drug addicts both in front and behind his back, etc. Naturally, Todd usually finds his boyfriends at circuit parties, like the rest of us. Saying that, Todd is actually a nice person and would deserve to be with somebody that treats him well, but he's also in this weird predicament where he's hormonally imbalanced and exclusively attracted to people on steroids who went to Mykonos last August, so I don't know what to tell him, really.

On this Wednesday Todd messages me:

"Konrad! I watched the video on Instagram of you giving yourself a haircut with your shirt off. Whom are you trying to impress?"

"Just trying to feel sexually desirable, to be honest. (Via reducing myself and prostituting my image)"

"Ooh, my ex is a hooker. I can get you tips."

"No, thanks. I have enough personal experience from bad exes now and I don't need other people's too."

"Interesting. Also my ex still asks me for money, so I haven't done very well."

"He can't be a very good hooker then. In any case, you definitely win."

"I don't want to win."

"One can win at losing. Not that I think you're a loser. Just attracted to the wrong men."

"Well, we have clearly established that. But I don't think that's going to change any time soon."

"You might bump into a good one by accident though?"

Todd doesn't think that he will bump into a good one by accident and now he has to go to the gym, so I move on to my next time zone.

12

I've been in San Francisco for about a month although sometimes it feels much longer and sometimes it feels like I got here yesterday; it's kinda hard to keep track of time when you're shut off in a room crushing and snorting tranquilisers and typing furiously in your journal and monitoring the online profiles of your ex and his new boyfriend and that's *all* you are doing. In this month I've not spoken to any real life people apart from Willa and her husband and I'm told that this isn't healthy, apparently, so I must go out and socialise. Willa puts me in touch with the only two other gay people she knows in the city, and we all know what a disaster it is when straight people put gay people together, but I message Graeme and Gene anyway and make plans to meet up. Graeme and Gene are a couple in their mid-40s. Willa has briefed them that I am currently a train wreck and they are nice and accommodating and willing to do whatever I want to do this evening. I choose my natural habitat: the club.

So we meet up and have dinner and then go to this club, which starts at 10pm. We have no drugs apart from some weed. Have you ever gone clubbing stoned? Don't.

The club is boring. Nobody's passing out in the corner and no circuit queens have even bothered to turn up, although there might be none in San Francisco, I don't know. Then a guy that I'm very interested in gets there with three other guys that I'm really not. A friend of Graeme and Gene's knows the four of them and takes me over to introduce me. Then he immediately leaves. All four people in my new group are very friendly, although their exact level of friendliness is inversely proportional to how attractive they are. I'm not very clever, but I do think this is how most humans work.

After a few minutes I leave my new friends and go back to my old friends, because sometimes I like to pretend that I have good manners.

Also so I can find out who's going out with whom in the group of four, because their interaction is confusing me. Graeme and Gene's friend tells me that the ones I'm not interested in are in a threeway relationship. Of course they are. Regardless, this is satisfactory.

Then Graeme and Gene and their friend decide to leave and go home because they are in their 40s and don't need this anymore and I decide to stay because at some point, somewhere, in my mid-20s, I lost all sense of what's wrong and what's right. So I go and join my new friends, who are now on the dancefloor with their shirts off in the middle of a whole big group of other people like the ones I have supposedly been trying to get away from. I spend the next seven hours with them, and then I go home alone.

13

I started off by feeling sorry for every poor soul who would see me in the gym, or on Grindr, or on Scruff, or on Adam4Adam, or on RealJock, or on OKCupid, or on Bigmuscle (I'm covering all bases) and decide to approach me. I kinda thought, there's no way that I'm not going to fuck over anyone that I meet in the next six months, at least. Then I went on a couple of actual dates and realised that I'm overestimating my importance once again. I can't do that to all these people. They're already fucked up. I'm not bringing anything new.

The avenues through which I'm supposed to meet all these men that I've typed above are not accidental. What are my strengths as a single, gay man, I thought? What do I have to offer? I have a decent body that photographs well and an overactive mind. I can also write words that level with people and resonate and make them feel like they can relate to me. Unfortunately I don't have the ability to do that in spoken word. Plus I'm socially awkward and don't do any activities and don't interact well and get tired of the outdoors very quickly.

Where does that leave me? Not in a great place. Bars are out. Social gatherings are out. Dinner parties are out. Networking events are out. Gay camping trips that include rafting are out (that's a thing, I'm not making this up). So what's left? The gym and online.

In the gym you don't have to say anything, you just have to work out and make studied eye contact (or not make eye contact at all, you know how it goes) and someone will come up and talk to you eventually, if they like your triceps. Especially in America. Oh America. How do they bring you up like that? So forward, upbeat and self-assured? I'm not really complaining. It's just that when you come talk to me, I'm a little bit scared.

Online you can throw some shirtless pictures on and hope for the best. Then when people message you and start a conversation, you can use your words. People tend to like that offbeat, outrageously straightforward manner that I use. It unsettles them, but intrigues them.

So I have to play to my strengths. And my strengths are being, writing, and not saying much. This makes for very promising online encounters and brief, awkward gym conversations. Then we meet for a date and actually have to spend real time with each other. And that's where the fun starts.

14

The unfortunate thing for the straight-acting, non-scene Berkeley or Stanford graduate bros currently living in the suburbs (or Palo Alto) who message me on any of the dating sites that I'm on, is that they don't realise that somebody who has six to eight visible abdominal muscles at any given point has not led a normal, balanced life so far and, more importantly, is not mentally stable. Still, they're so oblivious that they think I got those by participating in sport with my college buddies, or playing catch with extended family members on Sunday afternoon picnics in our grandparents' backyards, dressed in chinos and pastels, dirty blonde fringes flopping in the wind. Admittedly, the fact that I wear chinos and pastels in all my clothed pictures must also add to the confusion.

Overall, the compatibility between fallen circuit queens trying to escape the gay scene trajectory curve and non-scene upmarket bros is very, very low. Not only are these non-scene bros terrified of me, but I'm also appalled by them, because, you know, you're a grown man living in a liberal area, get over your issues.

On Friday evening last week, I get a text message from a non-scene bro in Palo Alto that I gave my number to on Adam4Adam maybe a couple of weeks ago. I'm going to call him John, because, well, what else would he be called? I don't know why John decided to message me now, because I don't follow any sports so I don't know what season just finished to empty his weekends, but in any case, this is a conversation that goes like this:

John: "What are you plans tonight/tmrw?"

Me: "Tonight I'm tired at home falling asleep. Tomorrow I have zero plans"

John: "K I'll be working tmrw, would u be able to come down to pa?"

Me: "I could come down"

John: "Grab a drink?"

Me: "Sure thing"

John: "Cool cool, what's ur drink/smoke of choice?"

Me: "Actually, I'll drink anything"

John: "Haha nice, smoke?"

Me: "What are you talking about? Weed? Yeah maybe"

John: "Just cigs"

Me: "No, I don't smoke cigarettes at all. You must think I'm very boring"

John: "Haha np. You wouldn't change ur mind on any of those, would ya?"

Me: "You want me to drive down to Palo Alto, so we can smoke cigarettes together?"

John: "Yeah can I corrupt you?"

Me: "I fear I'm a lot more corrupted than you think, John"

John: "Haha what do u mean?"

Me: "Never mind. So what are we going to do?"

John: "Haha u tell me"

Me: "Make out? Fuck? I don't know. I'm just throwing things out there. I'm sure even Palo Alto straight bros like to do these things from time to time"

John: "Haha I wanna see u be corrupted"

I'm not sure if this is suburb code for getting double-penetrated and I'm not prepared for that, so I ask:

Me: "How?"

John: "Smoke?"

Me: "Is that all?"

John: "We'll go from there, if ur down?"

Me: "Is smoking a big thing for you?"

John: "Ha nah. Just a turn on"

Me: "I'm not leaving the house for any less than snorting a line of coke off your cock"

Then John doesn't reply. Then I go to bed. Then it's Saturday evening 9.30pm and I text John again:

Me: "Hey, I just got here, where do you want to meet?"

Then John doesn't reply again. And I think it's over.

15

On Sunday evening I convince myself that I will have the first good night's sleep since January by starting taking inadvisable combinations of sedatives and sleeping pills early on, therefore building a gradual state of tranquility, hopefully slumber, that will take me through to the next morning. This plan is in contrast to my usual nonchalant method of trying to go without, then finding myself wide awake at 4am with a throbbing pain in my temples, running through the events of the last couple months. So at 9pm, I take 2mg of Xanax, followed by another 2mg at 10pm, followed by 5mg of Ambien at 11pm. Around midnight I start Ambien-posting on Twitter, until I suddenly pass out. At 2.30am, I wake up. I stay awake for an hour trying to figure out how it's possible to have an increased heart rate and a void feeling where my heart used to be at the same time.

Eventually I crush and snort 2mg of Xanax and 3.25mg of Zopiclone (that's half a pill) because it works faster than just swallowing them. At 5am, I wake up again and take half an Ambien (swallowed) and the other half of the Zopiclone that's left from earlier (snorted). At 6.45am I wake up again, go to the bathroom, take a mirror selfie demonstrating my abs looking particularly violent, because all these pills dehydrate the hell out of me, and post it on Instagram. I wait until it's had at least 350 likes before feeling like I'm worth something as a human being. This feeling lasts about two minutes, until somebody that I don't know leaves a snippy comment about me being self-absorbed. Then I turn my phone off and go back to sleep.

I wake up at 10.30am with a tolerable headache and down 2.5 litres of water before checking Facebook, Instagram, and Grindr. On Facebook there is universal uproar from a bunch of gay men who've spent their weekend sucking dick in club toilets and are now passing judgment on how trashy Miley Cyrus is, based on her performance at the VMAs. It seems that we're currently living in a society of very high moral standards; I guess I mustn't have noticed.

Late in the afternoon, I make my way to the gym. The gym might as well be empty apart from one guy. This guy is tall, in his mid-20s and on tons of anabolic steroids (good ones). He also seems to be on some sort of amphetamine or another, which I'm sure he refers to as his "pre-workout". Whatever. He's high. He's literally racing around the gym, eyes darting around maniacally, lifting weights in a state of frenzy. I recognise him as somebody I spoke to on Grindr earlier in the day. Soon enough, I have the honour and the privilege for his crazy eyes to fall upon me in real life too. From the moment he clocks me I become his new obsession.

His first course of action is to come stand behind me and lift his shirt up to check his abdominal muscles in the mirror. I am the person that I am, so that kinda works for me.

His second course of action is to sit on the bench next to me and pretend that he's working out there. He turns to me and mouths something that I don't hear, as I've got headphones on. I remove them and say:

"Hi, yes, we spoke on Grindr earlier, didn't we?"

This is not what he has just said. He has just said that he likes the tattoos on my arms. He proceeds to lift his shirt up again and show me his chest, sorry, "a tattoo on his chest", which is even worse than the ones I have. I say:

"That's really cool."

He then pretends to be aware that we spoke on Grindr, which is clearly not the case, as he pretends to remember information about me (where I moved from, what I do here), which I hadn't actually given him before. Despite all this unfortunate interaction he insists that we exchange numbers and of course I go along with it, because apparently I've learnt nothing from dating empty, beautiful vessels.

Right before I leave, amphetamine guy comes with me into the changing room to take my number. He points out my shirt, which randomly has "1987" written on it, and says:

"Dude, that's incredible, that's the year I was born. You know, we've got similar tattoos…your shirt shows my year of birth…you've got me all over you. Well, hopefully."

After this last comment I still give him my number, which suddenly makes me realise that I only have myself to blame for everything that goes wrong in my life and the state that I'm in.

We go on a date a couple of days later. The best part of the date is when I tell him I was born in Germany and he asks me what language they speak there, "is it German or Latin?"

The second best part of the date is when I tell him halfway through dinner that we have absolutely nothing in common, to which he seems to take offence, because you know, we have to sit there and pretend that we're soulmates and we're going to spend the rest of our lives together when all we want to do is fuck tonight and never see each other again.

After dinner I appear to disregard the fact that he's a complete moron and he appears to disregard the fact that I've been nothing but a dick to him, and we go back to his place together. He takes his clothes off and I stand there in awe for a bit, because his body is insane. I ask whether everyone reacts the same way when they see him naked for the first time and he says, "pretty much". Then we start making out. Then we're both naked in bed. Then I realise that this is actually the first time that I'm about to have sex with someone since my break up. And I start to cry. Or rather, I lose my hard on and I start to cry. The insanely hot guy doesn't understand what's happening exactly, so I sit there for the next ten minutes sobbing and give him a brief outline of my heartbreak, which I'm 100% sure is not how he wanted to be spending his Wednesday evening, and then I grab my clothes and leave.

AUGUST 2013

16

On Thursday morning it's raining and I'm sitting at home watching YouTube videos of pop songs that I like but I'm too embarrassed to own and play on my iTunes so I have to stream discreetly online instead. A message pops up on my Facebook from a guy called Lloyd M., whom I'm not friends with and know nothing about. Lloyd's profile picture is a selfie taken in his car. He is driving, but he's not wearing a shirt, nor is he wearing a seat belt. He looks like he's in his early 30s and he is unfeasibly handsome. In fact, he is so handsome that there must be something seriously wrong with him mentally, emotionally, or in any other possible covert way for him to be messaging random men on Facebook on a Thursday morning trying to make conversation with them. If there were nothing wrong underneath the surface with a guy who has that face, build, and overall demeanour, on a Thursday morning he would be making a speech at the World Economic Forum, or he would be addressing his alma matter as a graduation speaker before catching a flight to go back home and spend the evening with his slightly less handsome, equally high-achieving husband in their Chelsea loft. He is that superhumanly attractive. Doors don't just open up for him, doors fall off their hinges, come to life and set themselves on fire to let him through-level of attractive. He is Apollo, he is the ruler of Valhalla, he is an angel and a God.

Then again, it is the beginning of August and maybe he did address both the World Economic Forum and Harvard earlier in the year and I am, perhaps, being unfair. Then I click on his profile and see that he lives in Buffalo, NY, and the only education information provided goes up to a local college, but none of these red flags deter me from messaging him back, because now I have seen his traps and it's too late for me.

His message reads:

"How's it going out in Cali?"

Clicking into the conversation I see that he had also messaged me unprompted a few months ago, very soon after I moved to the US to ask, "How's LA?" but I guess I missed seeing that one back then, plus I wasn't really in the mood to talk to strangers at the time but right now it's all I do, so I write back and we continue talking and assessing each other as potential prospects.

Me: "It's going…OK. Getting used to it still, moved here recently"

Lloyd: "Where did u move from? That's awesome! Want to get out there myself."

Me: "Moved from London. So quite a big change."

Lloyd: "Very cool! Well good luck, by the looks of it you won't need it"

Me: "I don't know…everyone needs a bit of luck."

At this point he sends a friend request, which I accept, and then go and review his profile a bit more. We have a few friends in common who live in LA. One of them is Markus, the guy that Anthony is living with, and two others are Daniel and Rus, who are in a threeway relationship with X, an actually very famous movie star who's not openly gay to the public. I write to him more.

Me: "So you've never lived out here? You have quite a few friends in California though?"

Lloyd: "I haven't though hopefully someday soon. I have always wanted to live in south California. I've made a few friends there. How are you liking it so far?"

Me: "Well, I first moved to LA but I only stayed there for a couple months and I'm now living in San Francisco. I don't know where I want to be long-term."

Lloyd: "I'm in Buffalo. I grew up here but I travel a lot, love traveling. I love LA and every time I go I forget how good looking and gay that city is which is always fun but want a city with more substance. It KILLS being in Buffalo now though."

Then I think, oh my God, finally a guy who looks like that but also has some real substance and then I ask him what he does for work.

Lloyd: "I work in hospitality consulting and can transfer anywhere in the country but to be honest I hate it and when I get there I'm leaving the consulting world."

I don't know exactly what that means but it sounds really great to me right now, especially assessed alongside his jawline and the size of his biceps, so I write back something encouraging and then he asks me if I'm single and I say yes and then he writes back that he's dancing around the room at this news and then we leave it there for a bit and I go to the gym.

Later in the evening, he messages me again, because we are now fully preoccupied with each other, I guess, and the conversation goes like this.

Lloyd: "How come you moved all the way from London to Cali?"

The fact that he keeps referring to California as Cali is starting to bug me, because even I, having lived here for only a few months know that you're not meant to do that, but I suppose he doesn't know any better, and I write back.

Me: "Well, I don't want to get into the details, but I was in a long-term relationship in London and it ended by him starting something behind my back with someone else, and I didn't want to be in the same city as them anymore, so I felt like moving as far away as possible. And my Dad lives in CA, so I thought I'd try it out over here for a while."

Lloyd: "I feel sick reading that. That's why I can't live in West Hollywood. It's just a different mindset when it comes to relationships. So many of those hot 'glamorous' gays in the big cities like LA and London are just smoke and mirrors. They wear a good suit to project wealth, drive a nice car and they chase the next hot guy but after they cum what is left? Nothing."

Me: "Yeah, I don't know. What's most hurtful is that it all happened without me knowing anything. If someone feels like the love is gone and the relationship needs to end, he needs to be upfront about it."

Lloyd: "The cheating lying thing is the line I draw. You really think you should have to check up on your bf? Trust is crucial. And when that's gone it becomes so exhausting. I've been there."

Then I like him a little bit more, and then he says that he has to go to bed, because it is three hours ahead over there after all, and then I see that the rain has stopped for the first time today, so I take my iPod and go outside for a walk.

Halfway through New Order's *Technique*, I get a FaceTime call from Anthony in LA and Anthony knows that I don't talk on the phone and I've told him it's going to have to be an emergency if he calls me again, so this could possibly be an emergency or he may just be high and have forgotten again, but I answer either way.

Anthony is not exactly lucid and he launches into a story about having just been arrested. I guess that's entertaining enough so I listen to it and the story goes that he just left a wedding with Markus and Markus needed to pee really badly, so before starting to drive he stepped behind his car and started peeing on the street and Anthony thought that maybe he'd pee as well while he was waiting, so he walked two cars down and took his dick out and before he had had the chance to pee, a police car pulled up and shone lights on them and yelled at them and handcuffed them, and Anthony feels this was completely unfair as he hadn't even started peeing yet, but now he has a court date where he has to show up and be faced with one day in jail or a $2,500 fine or community service and he also gets a criminal record, but at least he was lucky enough that there wasn't a school in the area, because he would have also been registered as a sex offender if there was.

Then I also go to bed.

17

On Friday I wake up just before 8am and I decide that this is a good time to get up, because this is a time that somebody who might actually have somewhere to be might also get up and start their day.

I remember watching a German sitcom when I was very young, maybe twelve or thirteen, and this sitcom was about some very rich heiress who owned a bunch of factories or whatever and she never had to go to work, and there was this financial advisor guy she employed and he would sometimes come to see her at ten or eleven in the morning and he would wake her up, which always angered her, because her big thing, her life philosophy was that she just wants to have one luxury in life and nothing else: she wants to wake up whenever she feels like waking up, naturally, without anyone, alarm clock or other human being, interrupting her sleep. Because she thought that when you're asleep your soul leaves your body or something, and when you get abruptly woken up, your soul gets rushed into your body forcefully instead of returning peacefully, quietly, in its own time, and that's really destructive for you as a person. That was the sitcom's big joke, anyway. That she was so spoilt that she didn't have anywhere to be, nothing to interrupt her sleep for. And when I watched that it really bugged me. I mean it must have really bugged me a lot, I still remember it now twenty years later, because I thought, Oh my god, who is she? How can she possibly think like that? That's not just one luxury, that's just an impossible luxury, because it means you never have to go to work, you never have to go to school (I was twelve) you don't have an responsibilities or commitments to anyone. So in my head, this freedom of time, this endless, uninterrupted sleep was the impossible luxury, the ultimate sign of achievement and happiness, something so completely unattainable and unrealistic that it was used a comedic device in this low-budget German sitcom in 1992.

Now I wake up every day whenever I want without an alarm clock and I'm still really not quite sure where my soul is left wandering, surely I would be able to feel it if it were part of me somehow, so I guess whoever wrote that German sitcom in 1992 was wrong: waking up at your leisure and having nowhere to go, no responsibilities or commitments to anyone will not, by default, make you happy.

I have breakfast and think about leaving the house. Then I don't see a reason to leave the house, so I stay in.

Then a couple of hours pass and Willa asks me to meet her for lunch at this restaurant near her office, so I wear a button down shirt and chinos instead of a t-shirt and shorts even though it's rather warm and sunny, because Willa will be wearing her work clothes and I don't want to show up and embarrass her.

After lunch Willa goes back to work and I go back home, because I'm trying this new thing where I'm attempting to find some self-worth outside what my body looks like, so I've reduced my gym-going to only five days a week, and I stay there until 7pm talking to people via text or online and watching all seasons of *30 Rock* from the beginning and I don't give up even when it becomes stale.

Willa then texts me and says that she's going to the cinema to watch a movie with her husband and ask if I want to join them, so we text back and forth for about an hour trying to arrange this, then I decide that it's too much effort to go back all the way over there and I leave the house to go get some food at Whole Foods instead.

At Whole Foods I see a gentleman that I find very attractive, who's not just age appropriate (30+) but also doing a full-on grocery shop on a Friday night at 8pm, which means that he's perfect and ready to settle down. He is muscular and has tattoos, so I'm making the initial assumption that he's gay. Then I look at him for a few seconds and he catches my eye, then I walk away and pick up some food and walk towards the check-out and bump into him again on the way and we look at each other again, but perhaps only because I'm forcing it, and then I get to the check-out and pay for my teriyaki chicken bowl. I decide to take the long way out of the store so that I can see him a third time, and I see him a third time and we look at each other again, then he raises his arm and mouths something in my direction, which sends some very brief shockwaves through my stomach and heart, until I realise that he's actually trying to talk to somebody behind me – the person that he's here with – but I don't turn around to see if the person is male or female, gay or straight, age appropriate or not and I just exit the store quickly looking intensely on the ground.

When I get home, I eat my dinner and decide to go to the gym.

18

On Wednesday afternoon I'm at the gym and the really forward hot guy I hooked up with a few weeks ago who didn't know whether they speak German or Latin in Germany and I couldn't get it up for is also there, and I want to flirt with him again and I want to try hooking up with him again to prove something to myself, but he's well and truly done with me and he won't even catch my eye or say hi to me, and who can blame him really?

When I go home I start talking to Lloyd online again like we have been doing almost every day since those first messages we exchanged three weeks ago. A lot of these conversations have now even been on Skype, we're not just typing stuff. This is a full-blown made up long-distance love affair.

Today I really want to find out exactly how he knows the people he knows in LA, because I investigated on Facebook very thoroughly and found some pictures of him actually hanging out with Daniel, Rus, and X, who are in the three-way relationship. Well, the actor doesn't appear in the pictures because he doesn't appear in any Facebook pictures, but there are pictures of Lloyd hanging out with the other two.

I can tell this is a very sensitive subject and he doesn't want to talk about it, because from what I understand he met them online and they flew him out there and he had some sort of weekend sexual affair with them, and this goes against the whole image he wants to present of himself to me, where he's wholesome and moral as fuck and disapproves of gay lifestyles, promiscuity and those "glamorous city gays".

So I ask some very detailed questions and find out that this is exactly what happened two years ago, yes, but he's really regretted it and has moved on as a person and he was really young at the time and he was very naïve and he would never do anything like this again, and if I want to know actually, these people used him and they're really disgusting and he wants to have nothing to do with them anymore.

My initial reaction is, well, you're a 34-year-old man, you're fully aware of what you're doing, but I don't want to antagonise him too much because he's the closest I have to a potential boyfriend right now and I really need to have a boyfriend, no, I simply must have a boyfriend to prove to Brett and everyone else who knows me back in London and now in California that I'm not some kind of loser, who gets cheated on and dumped and can't find anyone to date him, so I give up on the interrogation, concede that perhaps was used and he has learnt his lesson and he has moved on now and is a different person, and then we jerk off on camera, cum, and hang up.

Then I start texting Anthony and asking him to ask Markus what he knows about Lloyd, because they're also Facebook friends, and this kind of gossipy backstabbing is right up Anthony's street, so within half and hour he's come back to me with some very elaborate stories and characterisations, but these go against my current plans to be Lloyd's boyfriend no matter fucking what, so I ignore them, get mad at Anthony and Markus and unfollow both of them on Instagram, for at least half an hour.

SEPTEMBER 2013

19

On Wednesday morning I get on an airplane and fly all the way across the continent to go visit Lloyd M. in Buffalo, NY. Last week I spoke to this guy in Miami that I know, who spent three months in London one summer a few years ago and we had a thing briefly and then he moved back to the U.S., and I asked him if he would be interested in hanging out again because I could easily fly to Miami and go on a date with him, but the Miami guy said that he's happy to hang out as friends but he's not interested in the romantic side of things anymore, so I decided to go to Buffalo instead.

I land at the airport and I'm really exhausted because this is a long trip and there is no direct flight from San Francisco to Buffalo, obviously, and then step outside and wait. Lloyd drives around the airport for half an hour or so and he can't find me and we have several conversations on the phone where I have to reassure him that I'm not catfishing him and I'm not the fat old guy he can see outside arrivals, because this has happened to him before, apparently, he was talking to a guy online for months and it turned out to be someone completely different, and as he tells me this I wonder how many people he has created long-distance online relationships with because I'm starting to lose count, and then he finds me.

I immediately fall in lust with him.

We drive to an airbnb apartment I've rented for three days because he didn't want me to stay at his house, his roommates are really messy, he said, and he's not on good terms with them and it's just best to have our own space, if I don't mind. I didn't mind so I paid a few hundred dollars for a horrible place near the water, and in fact I didn't know that Buffalo had a waterfront until I started looking, because I didn't know anything about Buffalo at all.

It's quite late in the evening by the time all this is done. We leave our stuff in the apartment and walk down to the water. Over the course of our communication in the past few weeks, I have found out that what Lloyd meant by "hospitality consulting" was that he works at a hut on the beach renting out kayaks and paddle boards to tourists in the summer months. It's still very unclear what he does in the winter months.

We sit on a blanket and make out a little bit but it's not very warm and I'm too tired from traveling so we only stay for half and hour and then go home to sleep. The next morning we get up, hang around for a bit and then he goes to work. I also do some work from home and then walk down to the lake again (I have now been informed that this is a lake and not the ocean as I may have originally thought) and take a picture sitting on the beach to prove to the social media world that I'm very active, not moping over my ex, Brett, at all, and moving on with my life. I don't actually say which beach I'm at when I post the picture on Facebook, because nobody has ever made anyone jealous by moving on with his life in Buffalo, NY.

On Friday morning Lloyd calls in sick at work and we spend the best part of the day lying in bed together. We also have sex for the first time. This will also be the last time we ever have sex, but I don't know that yet. In the afternoon we go to the beach, where I take a picture of him shirtless, just in his boardshorts, post it on my Facebook and tag him, adding the quote "This charming man" from the Smiths song. Possibly because of the fact that I currently have some goodwill behind me and people are feeling sorry for me, but also because he looks like a Roman god, this quickly becomes the most liked picture I have ever posted. The fact that he has over 2,000 friends on Facebook compared to my paltry 850, therefore catapulting my post to a massive new audience, may also have helped. He posts a picture of me on his own Facebook and adds the tagline, "Perfec day" [*sic*].

In the evening we go to a grocery store and buy ingredients for him to make dinner. I've told him that I can't cook to save my life, so now that we are planning our future together, he says that he'll take responsibility for always cooking for us. While he's cooking, I play music on my iPod to entertain us, because I'm the music guy and this is how we'll be doing things from now on.

What he cooks is more or less inedible and the dinner quickly turns into us getting pissed on three bottles of wine and empty stomachs. Even though our interaction has been perfect in the two days that I've been here, his mood noticeably shifts as he gets more and more drunk and he starts becoming irritable and short-tempered with me. Right around this point I stop drinking.

He decides to bring up our sexual history and asks how many people I've slept with. I tell him I don't exactly know, but it's a lot. He asks how many. I estimate between 100-150. He says that he finds that really disgusting and that all gay men are the same. I ask him how many people he has slept with and he insists it's "around as many as you can count on one hand".

I remind him that he's 34 years old, he has been out since he was 20 and I can already name seven people that he's had sex with: the guy he lost his virginity to, the two people he has dated for up to a year each, the guys in the threeway relationship who flew him to LA. And now me. And I'm pretty sure that this can't be the total count of people in fourteen years. He says that it is. I ask him what it matters anyway how many people we've slept with. We're here now, we like each other, and that's all there is to it.

He then decides to launch into an investigation about dating apps. He initiates this by shouting at me in an accusatory manner, "I bet you have Grindr." I tell him that yes, I do, and ask what is wrong with that. He slurs a brief tirade about gays in big cities and promiscuity and then wants to find out specific details, such as how many Favourite profiles I have currently saved on my Grindr and whether I send naked pictures of myself out. I tell him that I don't know how many Favourites I have and that, yes, I have sent naked pictures out before. At this point he gets so repulsed by me that he leaves the living room where we're eating and shuts himself in the bedroom. I am finding this a little difficult to understand.

After a while he comes out and says that we should just stop talking about this and move on. I say the same thing. This lasts about two minutes and then he asks specifically what pictures I've sent. I tell him that I don't understand what the problem is and what it has to do with him, anyway. I add that he, himself, has sent me naked pictures in the last month while we were talking, and he hadn't even met me yet. He says that I'm different, because he really liked me and then goes on to inform me that he's never ever downloaded Grindr on his phone and he hates all that social media bullshit anyway, he doesn't even do Facebook. I say that I find that hard to believe, seeing that he has thousands of friends on there, plus that's how he initially contacted me, and once again he walks away from me, this time to grab a pillow from the bedroom, come back, turn the light off, fall on the couch and shout that I can go to sleep in the bedroom alone before he passes out.

A few hours later in the middle of the night he walks sheepishly in the bedroom where I'm laying awake, apologises for losing his temper, kisses me on the lips and falls asleep next to me. We wake up, hang out at home for a bit being all sweet as if nothing happened the night before, and then he drives me to the airport to catch my return flight back to California.

20

Willa and her husband have gone away on some weekend trip somewhere and on Saturday afternoon my friend Chris, whom I met in the gym, comes over and we watch some terrible movie that he wants us to watch and do beauty treatments that we find in Willa's bathroom, and normally guys post Instagram pictures if they happen to be wearing some weird green mud face mask, because it's such an "interesting" juxtaposition of their masculinity with being in touch with their feminine side, but on this occasion I'd rather Willa didn't know we've been raiding her cabinets and using her stuff, so we don't post anything.

Later we go shopping for some clothes and some records and neither of us buys any clothes or records, but the shopping trip is not wasted because we do see an insanely hot guy and follow him around for a while, feeling inadequate. The things to know about this guy when we first see him from behind is that he has a big round ass, ridiculous calves like he's spent his entire life bicycle sprint racing (and I'm going to assume that he has, for extra thrills) and is wearing knee-length shorts, boat shoes with white ankle socks that are peeking out, and a large, thick sweatshirt that fits terribly and must be way too warm for this kind of weather (summer has finally arrived in San Francisco). This upsets me very much, because he's that hot despite disguising half his body underneath baggy, unflattering clothes and wearing white sports socks that don't make any sense, i.e. he's coming across as if he doesn't care how he looks at all. Chris points out that these straight guys' "I don't care what I'm wearing" looks are probably as contrived as the average gay guy's meticulously put together masc musc look and this makes me feel a little better, but only until the guy turns around and I see that his face matches the colour of his sandy blond hair: everything is practically monochrome, hair, tan, lips, with the only flash of colour coming from his soft, blue eyes. The guy is an Olympic sprint cyclist with a permanently applied Nashville Instagram filter and I am depressed again.

Chris and I then discuss how pathetic it is that we're still crushing on these hot, young guys (we're both almost in our mid-30s and the guy is maximum 26) and wonder whether it will ever go away or we'll end up like those old men who try to talk to young dudes in the gym and connect with them on a bro level and it's embarrassing for everyone involved, because the old gay guys try to act all young, but in fact they do the young things that were cool in their time, like wear tight Abercrombie t-shirts or have tribal tattoos, and I don't know whom I'm kidding, I'll definitely be one of those old guys.

Then as we're still walking around I get a text message from Lloyd, asking what I'm up to and I tell him that I'm hanging with my friend Chris, and Lloyd says that he can't stop thinking about me and I say the same and then Lloyd adds that his feelings are very strong and he thinks that he loves me and I say, wait a minute, I believe that "being in love" with somebody is different than "loving" somebody and the latter comes with time, so which one does he mean? And Lloyd M. writes back without missing a beat that he's both in love with me and he loves me and I show to Chris and Chris says, is that the guy you just visited in Buffalo just last week, and I say, yes, and Chris says, OK.

21

On Monday there isn't that much happening, because it's like every other day, and for that reason I am sitting here in Willa's living room and chatting to Anthony back in LA. This is a real emergency, apparently, and for that reason he tried to FaceTime me a couple times but I didn't want to do that, so we made a compromise to text instead. Anthony's emergency is from his Sunday Funday outing in WeHo's gay bars yesterday and I know already of course that this isn't an emergency at all, but I'm here and I'm willing to listen, because what else do I have to do?

Anthony's situation right now is this: he has stopped working as a go-go dancer. He is still living with and living off Markus. Markus and he have broken up and are just friends currently.

Anthony has only been in LA for a few months and he's young and attractive and he's still stuck at that stage where he thinks that all these silly gay adventures that he finds himself engaging in have never happened to anyone in the history of the universe before and will never happen again, and honestly his life is so complicated right now that he ought to write a book about it, or so he says. Also he's tired of all this drama and the sleeping around and he wants to find a serious boyfriend and go out much less, if at all, but everyone is really shallow and not relationship-orientated and they just want to have sex with him and then move on to the next person and why can't he find someone who is as mature and over it as he is and wants the same thing?

So Anthony starts telling me his story from Sunday and the best way that he feels he can possibly deliver the whirlwind of events and emotion that is his life right now is through a list. And he types:

"1. I'm sick

2. Ran into five past hookups

3. Markus was also out and he was a shitshow

4. Left to go hook up with Eric and I couldn't get off so I left

5. Then I went back to Here bar"

I write back:

"1. You should probably drink less

2. You and everyone else who went out, I'm sure

3. I'm going to stop commenting completely if you keep making such obvious statements

4. [Expressionless emoji]

5. Mess

I don't like using the word "mess" but I understand from the boys of the Popjustice messageboard that it's multipurpose and can be inserted anywhere to convey disapproval with a camp, raised eyebrow and I think that someone like Anthony would appreciate this right now.

Then Anthony hasn't finished with his list of high emergency events that happened yesterday, so he continues:

"6. Victor cornered me and wanted to know why he wasn't good enough for me

7. This random kept trying to make out with me and then found me on FB this morning

8. I talked to Aaron and he wants to get together this week [emoji of sassy brunette girl with arms crossed in front of her body to convey refusal]

Then I reply:

"6. Who is Victor? (I just woke up, sorry if this is obvious)

7. This sentence can be said by 840 people in WeHo this morning

8. This sentence can be said by 840 people in WeHo this morning"

Then Anthony writes:

"You are so witty in the morning", because I didn't take his stories seriously enough and then I write:

"I'm sorry, I just don't see any emergencies there. It sounds like you're going through a very predictable phase of being young, in a big city, relatively new to the gay thing and having a crazy old time going out / socialising / hooking up, which is punctuated by feelings of remorse when you look back on it the next day, then repeated ad infinitum. It's all very normal and will be your life for the next ten years [heart kiss emoji]"

Then Anthony doesn't say anything back and then I start messaging Lloyd instead who continues to say all the right things to me and is completely ready for serious commitment and over the gay scene and I'm so lucky that he came into my life to save me and none of this will ever end up in a complete disaster, not at all.

During the phonecall Lloyd suggests that we play a game and this is a game he calls "hypotheticals". For hypotheticals, one of us has to come up with an imaginary scenario that might occur when we're boyfriends and living in the same city and the other person has to respond with how he would react if this scenario came to be. This, apparently, is a way for us to find out more about each other.

In reality, this quickly goes down the usual route where Lloyd asks me a question, I answer it as honestly as I possibly can and he quickly gets mad at me because my answer doesn't fit within the moral, anti-gay scene, heteronormative ideals he so dearly holds close to his heart. For example, his first question regards my training habits. Lloyd is concerned that I'm too obsessed with going to the gym and thinks that this might be detrimental to my social life and personal relationships, so he presents me with the following hypothetical:

We are both living in California. It's a Wednesday evening and one of his very close friends from back home is in town for one night only and wants to meet up with us and go have dinner, spend some time together. I have worked all day and usually I would go to the gym in the evening, but what do I do on this occasion? Do I still go to the gym and miss hanging out with him and his friend, or do I skip the gym for one day?

I pause and think for a second and answer that I would probably try to go to the gym quickly and then go meet them and do whatever they want to do, but Lloyd doesn't like that answer at all and says that I'm like all the other gays who are only focused on going to the gym and maintaining their good looks or whatever, and he's sorry, but he's not like that and for him family and friends always come first, and then I panic a bit and tell him that he's right, I probably shouldn't care so much about going to the gym every day and I don't want to be *that* person, and then I retract my initial answer and say that I would totally skip the gym and go hang out with him and the friend.

After a few more hypotheticals I start discussing living in San Francisco with him and tell him that I don't feel like this is where I would want to stay in the long-term because it's just a whole different scene of people, plus I don't really like the weather at all and if I'm going to have to walk around wearing long-sleeves in the summer all the time I might as well move back to London, which I love, and explain that I'm starting to think about going back to LA and trying that out again. And I say that this time things might be different because if he also moves to LA with me, I won't have to do any of the gay scene stuff that I was doing before, because I will have a boyfriend and it will be a completely different experience. And Lloyd says that, you know what, he's not such a big fan of LA and LA gays in particular like he's told me before, and he thinks that everyone over there is "so Hollywood" and that they're not good people, but at the end of the day if I want to move he'll move wherever I want, he'll do that for me.

Then he asks me who I think are the five best looking gay guys in the LA scene and I have no idea what to tell him or why he's asking me that, and then eventually we say goodnight and hang up.

OCTOBER 2013

22

There will be a key moment in your life when you're 33 and have started to lose your looks and some of your wit and you haven't been as successful or rich as you once thought you might be and you haven't even been around your family that much since you were 16 and you've made several wrong decisions which have left you living alone in a new continent surrounded by people who either don't know you that well and don't care about you or know you pretty well but care even less and you'll be fully aware that the nearest people who truly love you live back in London where you came of age 5,400 miles away... when you will consider that this is it, things couldn't possibly get worse, you've seriously reached the bottom and the only possible way is up. Then you'll get to the gym on a Tuesday afternoon for an intense leg workout and the left headphone in your cheap Sony headphones will have inexplicably stopped working. And this is something that you're going to have to deal with.

23

On Thursday evening I get on my bike and I go to the gym and the best thing that happens at the gym is that right at the end, when I'm doing my sit ups, some genuine bro with pale, white skin, a very nice straight nose and spectacular biceps comes and sits next to me and starts doing crunches, then gets his phone out and orders a pizza for delivery.

I have no idea where these bros are going to stop, where they're willing to push the limits to, but they can rest assured that I will always fall for it. I also don't even know how they come up with these inventions. Ordering a half Hawaiian, half Meat Lovers pizza with extra cheese in the gym, mid-abdominal crunch. They are killing me.

Then I go home.

In the middle of the night I wake up with a bad dream about Brett and his new boyfriend, which has become a new nightly routine, and stay up for a couple of hours, during which I make a sandwich, obsess, watch a couple episodes of *Frasier* and freak out some, before passing out again around 7am.

Then next day I meet up with Chris, still my only gay friend in San Francisco, and we go bowling, because this is something that counts as a sport, barely, and I will try every sport until I find one that I am not terrible at, so that I possibly reassure myself a little bit about my own masculinity.

During this bowling adventure we talk about vacations, pool parties in big bungalows in the California countryside where people have only water and pills to sustain them, and the futileness of existence despite great wealth, because what else would two white, North American, adult gay men with no real problems talk about, and then we get to relationships.

I update Chris on Lloyd and tell him that we are now officially boyfriends and that I'm really putting the pressure on him to move to

LA with me as soon as possible, because I've definitely made up my mind that I want to go back there. I also tell Chris that sometimes I have second thoughts about Lloyd, because he cannot seriously be as pure and perfect as he makes it out to be, plus I've caught him out on a couple of lies already that concerned major things like his job and his previous relationships, etc, but he weighs over 220lbs and it's all muscle, plus he wears button down shirts, visors and boat shoes and has light eyes and is therefore a god, not to mention that he's insolent as fuck and often goes whole days ignoring my calls, but then comes back and likes all my Instagram pictures, which means that he's a sociopath who loves games and consequently made for me.

Chris asks me whether I would like perhaps to date somebody for once who's not completely wrong and trying to blackmail my emotions, and I ask why I would want to do that. Chris says that maybe that way I will live a perfectly peaceful life without heartbreak and the only reply that I can think to that is that I want heartbreak, I want emotional highs and lows that will torment me, I want intense, passionate love affairs that make me want to kill myself and the other person or abduct them and keep them locked up in my basement, but nothing in-between, I want surface, trophy boyfriends that elevate my status and make me self-loathe equally, I want to feel.

Then the bowling comes to an end and I'm not very good, though I might just need to keep practicing, and we leave.

24

In the early hours of Wednesday morning I'm lying in bed watching the final of the *Great British Bake Off* and then when that's over and I still can't sleep I put on the 1963 film *Contempt* and halfway through that my sleeping pills finally kick in and I pass out. I wake up in the late morning and finish watching the film, then do some work and go to the gym. In the evening I go out and pick up three pizzas with Willa and her husband and then come home and eat them, though I did forget to buy Coke and I really like drinking Coke with my pizza.

It takes a good couple of hours to get through this and I continue eating way past the point where I'm completely full, but I'm doing this thing at the moment where I'm trying to enhance my importance and impact on this planet by increasing my physical mass, seeing that this seems to be the only thing anyone cares about. I could have spared you the previous twenty-seven words by just typing, "bulking", but I don't feel I can pull off that term for myself as it depends on results and I don't feel confident enough that I will achieve them.

On Thursday I go and have lunch at my third favourite restaurant in San Francisco and then I go to the gym. There are two very important things that happen at the gym.

The first important thing is that the most beautiful man who has ever lived on the entire planet turns up. I will skip the physical description, but it suffices to say that any human male that I ever come across from this point onwards will be judged and compared against this gentleman, because I really needed to increase my physical standards even more, guaranteeing that I will die miserable and alone.

The second important thing that happens in the gym is that when I go to the locker room after to get changed and leave, two bros are stood there talking and those two bros are: 1) the pizza bro from last week who was doing sit-ups and simultaneously ordering a pizza for delivery on the phone, 2) another bro I see every evening who has a blond beard, nice muscles and exclusively listens to some stupid hardcore metal shit that makes him head-bang consistently throughout all his workouts. The conversation between those two bros, who seem like they haven't spoken before goes like this:

Pizza bro: "You look so big, bro."

Hardcore bro: "Thanks man, I been bulking, so."

Hardcore bro after a brief pause: "Do I really look bigger?"

Pizza bro: "Yeah, you look huge."

Hardcore bro: "Thanks man. And I haven't even been training as much as I want."

Pizza bro: "How many days do you lift?"

Etc, etc.

Then I leave before they start making out and punch myself in the face for not being man enough to ever speak to either of them, though perhaps they don't want to speak to me because they can tell I'm gay and they prefer their homosexual banter safe, heterosexual, and leading nowhere.

When I come out of the gym I text Chris and tell him exactly what just occurred in the gym (both with the most handsome man in the world and the locker room bros) and finish my message with: "EVERYOBE IS BULKIN. EVERYONE IS A BRO. EVERRYONE IS PERFECT. I WANT THEM ALL".

The Chris texts back: "Can we just get them all together (possibly drug them if we have to) and have an orgy. And why do you disappoint me by not getting a pic of this beautiful man?"

Me: "I thought about it but his beauty was paralysing. I didn't want to do anything that would infiltrate his perfect existence."

Chris: "If you see him again, you must."

Me: "I'll try. I'm so glad we're ahead of the curve with our bulking though. I feel like for once, we've tapped into a real trend early on and we're making good progress."

On Friday night I go to the cinema with Chris to watch *This Is Where I Leave You* and I dare him to ask for two tickets to *"Dis Where I Leave You"* but he doesn't and this really disappoints me, because I know that a hardcore bro would.

After the film I go back home and talk to Lloyd on the phone and announce to him that I'm moving back to LA in less than a month, but I will be living on the beach this time, and insist that he also moves there before the end of the year to be with me, otherwise we're going to have to break up.

NOVEMBER 2013

25

On Saturday I move into my new place in Venice. It's a one bedroom flat at the top of a small, two-floor complex, three blocks from the beach. There is a courtyard in the middle with a small swimming pool, the building manager lives on the ground floor with his girlfriend, who has pink hair and thinks she's a punk, and a lot of the residents keep surfboards on their balconies. I think I like it.

The first thing I did was get Wi-Fi installed. I had the technician come in yesterday, before I even moved in. I would rather have had Wi-Fi than running water. Today my mattress also arrived and I just put it on the bedroom floor. I don't have a bed yet. The mattress is a Queen size. I might have gotten a King size, because of my ridiculous sleeping problems and always wanting to move around, but Lloyd complained that with a King mattress we would be spending the night too far from each other and we wouldn't be able to cuddle. So I didn't.

I have zero other furniture. I'm waiting for Lloyd to arrive, so we can go and buy everything together. He has agreed to quit his job and leave everything behind and move to LA for me next month.

My kitchen window is facing inside the building, and across the courtyard I can see the kitchen window and front door of the flat directly opposite mine. This evening, they are keeping the front door open. There is quiet music coming out of their living room. I understand that a young couple in their late 20s lives there, and tonight they are having a party. I stand in my kitchen with the lights off and look across for a while. It would seem that it's the boyfriend's birthday. He is short, with dark hair and glasses and he's dressed for a climate much colder than this. He looks very Jewish. The girlfriend is the exact opposite. She is blonde and surfery and looks like she just came straight from the beach. In the half hour that I stand and watch in the dark, a few of my other neighbours walk over to the flat, some carrying gifts or bottles and join the party. Most people that I see are up to 35 or so, and almost all of them are couples. Possibly one day soon these people will be my friends.

I have nothing to do this evening, so I take my bike and ride over the two blocks to the beach. The Venice Boardwalk is busy as ever, but as I ride north on the bike path, up towards Santa Monica and past the pier, it gets a lot quieter and a lot darker. Soon the only light around me comes from the headlight on my bike, and the only people I come across are evening joggers or small groups of skateboarder kids practicing and getting stoned on the beach. I'm listening to a playlist with old songs that made me sad back when I was very young, when I was still living in Berlin, by bands like The Smiths, Suede, and Gene, hoping for a similar feeling now at 33. This works pretty well, with added layers of sadness because I now know a lot more about the passing of time and empty lives, and I soon reach a very satisfactory level of nearly tearful nostalgia. This is probably my most content emotional state, especially when it's caused by circumstances I've deliberately created to trigger it, like I'm doing now, as opposed to uncontrollable situations that happen around me and I fall victim to.

My ride lasts an hour or so. I think about Brett a lot, think about his new life and wonder if he's happy and whether he actually ever thinks of me, if he misses me sometimes.

On the way back, on the same bike path closer to Venice again I ride by ten million dollar properties right on the ocean front and these are my favourite properties on the planet, so I slow down to look inside. People's lights are on, they're home for the evening and I see some of them in their kitchens, in their living rooms, couples and families and friends with their perfect lives in their perfect homes right by the ocean. I text Chris and complain about them a little bit, and ask why our lives aren't perfect like that. Chris writes back and he says, do you not think that maybe some people look at you and think you have a perfect life? Maybe people who just see your Instagram? And I say, yeah, maybe they do. And Chris says, right, and look at how shitty your life is, you idiot, and I take the point and I go back home.

From there, I give Lloyd a call. It's 1am on the east coast. I know that he's gone out. He doesn't answer his phone the two times that I call and finally calls me back an hour later. He's driving back home, he says. He didn't answer before because he'd forgotten his phone in a friend's car. He's very, very drunk and decides to launch into a story about the U.S. Government and all the secrets that they're keeping from us, something about aliens, something about terrorism, and then a lot more stuff about aliens, then we eventually hang up when he's arrived home.

26

I haven't spoken to Anthony, my scene friend, since I moved back to LA. I don't think I even told him I was moving back. I still have those irrational complexes about the gay scene being the root of all evil and the reason why my last relationship fell apart and I had to move all the way over here, and I'm not ready to be part of it again. I fear I may have become one of those self-loathing semi-closeted gay guys you talk to on Grindr who live in the suburbs surrounding big cities and stop talking to you when you tell them you live in a more central, gay area. This is all sorts of fucked up, because in reality I think those guys are as disgusting as the scene ones, only in a much different way, but now I have found a way to combine the negative attributes of both those groups in myself, and become truly the worst.

On Saturday afternoon, Peter Henderson comes over to the beach and picks me up to go on a hike at a place called Point Dume in Malibu. This is the first time I've met Peter. He's somebody my friend Chris from San Francisco put me in touch with, and I guess I'm going to try to be his friend so that I don't spend every single minute in Southern California alone until Lloyd arrives to save me. The hike goes well. Peter seems nice enough and as a bonus I am not sexually attracted to him, which is very promising for our potential friendship. When Peter gets tired of hanging out with a depressive misanthrope on the west side, he goes back to Hollywood where he lives and I go back to my flat in Venice.

I talk to Lloyd and tell him that I went on a hike with a new friend and Lloyd tells me that it sounds like I went on a date actually and gets mad at me and then I reassure him that it absolutely wasn't a date and what I'm supposed to do, lock myself in the house and not talk to anyone? That's what I do most of the time anyway. Then Lloyd calms down a little bit even though he's still not happy, he says, and asks me how I'm finding LA anyway now that I'm back there and I say that I guess it's OK but it will be a lot better when he's there with me next month and then Lloyd says he can't wait either but he'd rather I didn't live in such a gay area as Venice. I tell him that Venice is not a gay area specifically and what is he talking about, and he says that he's heard that Venice is gay enough and if it were down to him he would be living somewhere like Manhattan Beach, and I say, well OK, I guess I'm gayer than he is and he's a genuine masc non-scene bro and he can move to Manhattan Beach if he likes when he gets here. Then he says that he might, asks me again who the top 5 sexiest guys in LA are, if I were to make a list, I fail to come up with any names because a) I don't care, b) I'm blindly in lust with him and no one else seems attractive, and we hang up.

In the evening of my second Saturday back in LA I sit at home and take a few bumps of ketamine and listen to the album *Halfaxa* by Grimes all the way through and then I get in my car and go grocery shopping in a supermarket that's not the nearest to my house, but the second nearest, because I wanted to drive. When I come out of the store with all my bags I put them in the trunk and then I sit in my car for a bit in the parking lot and it's after 10pm and I cry for a bit, because this is all I ever wanted to have, someone to go grocery shopping with me on a Saturday night and I guess here I am and I don't, then I get over this and drive home.

27

On Friday early evening, after almost a week's drive across the country, Lloyd finally arrives in LA. I can now start leading a very happy existence, seeing that he is my only source of happiness. I go downstairs to greet him and let him in. He's even more attractive in real life than I remember. I help him carry his stuff upstairs from his car, and then offer him his favourite beer, a huge supply of which I bought to welcome him, because I am emotionally subservient when I am in love and want to make him happy. He tells me that he doesn't want to drink it right now; in fact he's considering that he will stop drinking alcohol for at least a year now that he's moved here, because he really wants to turn his life around, become successful, stop falling victim to all the distractions and young behaviour that he's been trapped in, not to mention that it's gay people who go to all the bars and clubs and are part of the scene that get wasted all the time and take drugs, and he doesn't want to be one of them. I say, oh OK then, and put the beer back in the fridge. We kiss each other for a little bit, but then he says he's really tired and wants to sleep very early, which makes sense, so he showers and goes to bed. I walk down to Abbot Kinney and have dinner by myself and also bring some home for him in case he wakes up and gets hungry.

On Saturday after we wake up I make breakfast and he starts unpacking and putting his things away. I've left half of all closet and storage space empty for him. When most of that is done (he hasn't brought many things at all) I attempt to make out with him and possibly fuck, but he tells me that he hasn't been to the gym in a week because he was driving across the whole country to get here and he body looks like shit at the moment so I'm not allowed to see him naked, nor am I allowed to touch him, so we'll have to wait. I reassure him that his body looks fine to me and question what possible difference five days of not working out could possibly have made, but he is adamant and I give up. Once he gets back into his gym routine and rebuilds his body, he says, we can get naked.

Peter then comes over to meet us for lunch. We drive over to Main Street in Santa Monica and sit at a place called The Gallery. I am immensely happy that I now have a boyfriend and a friend who want to do boring stuff like that with me. Why was I so upset over Brett leaving me? Clearly we wanted different things and were never meant to be together. Halfway through the lunch, Lloyd says that he's gonna go over to LA and meet up with some friends. I ask who these friends might be and he says, Daniel, Rus, and X, which makes sense as they are the only people he knows in the city. Somehow I don't particularly like the fact that this is happening and I'd love to go with him and check the situation out, but I don't really want to be a highly paranoid, suspicious and controlling boyfriend (even though I am) so I let him go and stay on the west side with Peter. A couple of hours later, Peter also leaves.

Around 8pm, and having not heard anything from Lloyd all day, I text him to see what he's up to. At this point I'm so bored and alone that I want to go meet him and even go out with him in West Hollywood if that's what he wants. He texts back half an hour later with the following message:

"Heyy bub im with myfreinds how;s yo"

Even for someone expectedly inarticulate that seems a bit much, so I text back with a simple, "What"? He doesn't respond and then about an hour later, I give him a call. He answers from a place where really loud music is playing and I can hardly hear him. I make something out about Daniel, Rus, X and I ask where he is and if I can come join them. I can't hear any more of his answers and then the call drops. "The call drops" is code that I use on myself to make the fact that he hung up on me sound better. I text him immediately quite furious and ask what the hell he's thinking leaving me by myself all day on his first weekend in LA and going to hang out instead with the people he's been having orgies with in the past. He texts back with:

"rOrgies? Goodbye Konrd"

I spend the next hour calling his mobile and texting him but I don't get any response and then eventually decide to leave the house and go to the gym. My blood is boiling. In the parking garage in the gym I'm so distracted and mad that I drive my car into a pillar while taking a left turn and create a big dent on my door, and then I work out.

Lloyd comes back home at 11.30am the next morning. He looks like death. Whom am I kidding, he still looks like some sort of god and I would kill every living relative I have outside my Mum to a) have sex with him, and b) be seen out in a public place with him. He says that he's sorry and that he got upset with me because I was making accusations while he was just out, spending time with his friends. For some reason he got really drunk, he says, and he thinks that somebody probably spiked his drink with drugs, because it doesn't make any sense otherwise. He really didn't drink all that much. I say that that's bullshit, he started drinking at midday and it makes perfect sense how he would have gotten so drunk by the evening, add that this is a perfect start to his plan to turn his life around and become more responsible in LA, and ask if he thinks his parents would be proud of him. This seems to touch a nerve and he jumps up from my bed where he's been hiding under a blanket because he's hung over as hell and mostly unable move and he tells me that that's it, we're done and he's moving out, and makes a half-hearted attempt to grab a bag and throw his stuff in. I start crying and begging him to forgive me, I didn't mean what I said, so he forgives me and goes back to bed.

I suddenly recall that he once told me during our extensive long-distance interaction that he gets particularly horny the next day after a big night out after his hangover has subsided a bit, so I leave him to sleep for a couple of hours, then get naked and get into bed with him. I start pulling his clothes off and trying to kiss him. At this point I realise that he's not wearing any underwear, even though he's still wearing the clothes he was wearing when he left yesterday. There are two possibilities here, either he left his underwear somewhere in the last thirty-six hours that he's been out or he left to go to the gay bars without wearing any underwear to start with, and I don't know which scenario is giving me the biggest aneurism, but either way I choose to ignore the fact for now and continue my attempt at acquiring a sex life. He regains full consciousness for a moment while I'm sucking his dick, which is surprisingly hard, just to push me away. I leave him to sleep and go jerk off in the bathroom thinking of his perfect, unconscious body laying on my bed and then spend the rest of the day taking turns between reading a book in the next room and going to look at him to regain inspiration and jerk off again while I wait for him to wake up. By 6pm when he emerges from the bedroom, I have cum four times.

DECEMBER 2013

28

On Monday I have about half a day's work to do. Lloyd wakes up and sits in the opposite side of the living room looking for jobs on his laptop. He has been here for over two weeks now and even though he has joined a gym again and started working out, our sex life remains elusive. He has also taken to building a barrier comprising two pillows between us when we sleep, which is a far cry from the days when he was asking me all the way from Buffalo not to buy a king size mattress because we wouldn't be able to cuddle, but I fear that at this stage there isn't even a remote correlation between what was being said then and what is happening now.

The gym he has joined is a different one to the one I go to, it's all the way in LA and he has to drive over 25 minutes to get there with no traffic, but he told me that he prefers to work out somewhere else because working out is really important to him and he wants to go there, get in the zone, and do his own thing, plus we can't be joined at the hip and do everything together just because we're boyfriends. In fact, he said, relationships are stronger when two people have their own personal lives and just get together to enjoy each other's company whenever they want to. That's the sign of a good relationship, he said. Well we now don't work out together, we don't go out together, and we don't have almost any physical contact, so our relationship must be pretty fucking solid.

On this Monday, his job hunt remains on a very perfunctory level, which at least shows a sign of consistency that I've really come to admire about his character in the time that he's spent here, and he soon switches to his favourite daytime activity: making a music playlist to accompany his afternoon workout. This is an activity that takes up three or four hours every day. It seems to be extremely important for the music that he listens to in the gym to change every day and it's meticulously selected and put together, so much so that I really find it hard to imagine how he could also fit an actual job in his day. Perhaps that is why he is avoiding getting one.

When that's done and I'm finally spared continuous bursts of brief segments of songs he's trying out coming from the tinny speakers of his shitty old laptop, he continues to sit there, this time playing with his phone. The phone starts buzzing at an alarming rate, indicating an influx of text messages that I, personally, have only experienced when I'm trapped in a group iMessage with seventy-five other people. When I ask him who's sending all these messages, because I'm a very open-minded, non-controlling boyfriend if I'm anything, he responds that he's decided to text everyone who appears in his Contacts as a first name entry only and he can't remember where he met them, to enquire about their connection. Yes, that is my brand new boyfriend who refuses to have sex with me hitting up all his previous hook ups. Before all my blood rises to my head I decide to take a break and go outside to pick up some lunch.

When I come back with food for both of us, I find him bursting his gym playlist from the living room stereo and dancing around. We sit down at the dining table to eat, but as soon as we've started *Gas Pedal* by Sage The Gemini comes on and this causes him to exclaim "woooooooh" very loudly, put his fork down, raise his arms up in the air and start grinding heavily on the chair. The combination of his exposed blond hairy armpits, his biceps which he's flexing above his head and the fact that he's grinding so hard that it's a genuine miracle the chair doesn't disappear inside his enormous, muscular ass leaves me so intensely horny that it becomes almost impossible to breathe. Any doubts that I ever had about this relationship are put to the side. I will do anything for this guy as long as I live. He can stay here at my place forever. He can continue being repulsed by me and avoid touching me, but I will continue feeding him and sheltering him as long as I'm given the privilege of being allowed to look at him this close up. He is a god.

Because of my horny delirium, I make another futile attempt at physical contact. I tell him that he looks really hot and ask him if he'd like to fuck. He continues to dance and tells me that I look hot too, but

I'm so obsessed with sex and need to chill out a little bit. Relationships are not all about sex, he says. I say that I agree but relationships are a little bit about sex, and we're not having any sex at all. The song changes to *Wiggle* by Jason Derulo. He takes his tank top off, because he's a cruel bastard, stands up, walks over to my chair and sits on my lap, where he starts grinding on my dick.

"So you want to fuck?" he says.

"Yes."

I put my arms around him and start kissing his chest. He leans back, still grinding on my crotch and I kiss his stomach then pull him back up to face me and start making out with him.

No more than five seconds later, he stands up, stops the music and puts his shirt back on. I ask him what the hell he's doing. He says that he's running late for the gym and we can continue this later. He throws his gym stuff in a bag and leaves. He comes back home hours later, just before 9pm, with no explanation as to where he's been and we don't really talk to each other until we go to bed with a pillow fortress between us.

I'm still awake at 3am. I finally get up because this sleep thing isn't happening for me, get dressed and go outside for a walk. It's very cold though, so instead I just sit on the steps at the building entrance and listen to a short playlist I've made alternating songs from the albums *Overgrown* by James Blake and *Cupid Deluxe* by Blood Orange.

When I go back up, I sit on the side of the bed and wake Lloyd up. I must be visibly upset. "What's wrong, bubba?" he says. I tell him that I don't know what's going on and that I'm really unhappy. I ask him to tell me whether he likes me at all anymore. I say that I know relationships are not all about sex, but he must be able to see that this is a problem. There's no intimacy between us. He sits up to indicate that he's fully present and willing to participate in this forced heart-to-heart. He nods his head slowly, lowering his eyes, in a move that's meant to convey he understands and is equally upset. I ask him to tell me what is wrong then. If there's anything I can do to help. He doesn't speak for a few seconds and then he says that he thinks he has developed some sort of fear. He says that he can't even remember when he last had sex with anyone. I remind him that he had sex when I visited him in Buffalo back in August. He says, oh yeah, he can't even remember when he last had sex with anyone apart from the time I visited him in Buffalo back in August. Because he'd been living there for so long, he says, and he was so unhappy with his life, he stopped thinking about sex completely. Plus there really wasn't anyone around to date. Apart from that one time with me, he hasn't had sex in over a year. Maybe two years even, he can't remember. Now he's built up a wall, and it's difficult to let anyone in. He says that he finds it really upsetting, if I must know. I tell him that I wasn't aware of that and that I understand. I tell him that we can take it slow and that I'm there for him. He says great, let's go back to sleep now and I move over to my side of the bed.

29

On this Saturday afternoon, three weeks after having lived with me, Lloyd is gracious enough to allow me to go to the same gym as him and work out at the same time, albeit not together. This is good enough for me. When we finish out workouts, we decide to go in the swimming pool area and maybe swim for a bit, maybe use the steam room. In preparation for this, as soon as I'm done with the weights, I go into the gym locker room toilet and quickly jerk off. This should provide me with some temporary peace of mind and the ability to co-exist with Lloyd in his swimming shorts without being driven completely crazy with desire, because, as has been pointed out several times, he is a god.

We swim a couple laps and then both go into the steam room. Because he is heartless or a moron, but most likely the perfect combination of both, he asks me when the last time was that I used a steam room. I say that I don't actually remember, it's probably several years ago, and I don't particularly like it, if I go to a pool I usually just swim and get out. I ask him the same thing, because that's what he wanted. He says that it was a few months ago when he was visiting DC, and he says that in a very gleeful way that makes his whole face light up. I am masochistic enough to ask what thrilling memories he may possibly have from that steam room in DC and he replies that something happened there. I press on, even though I know where this is going and where this is going is not very beneficial for the arteries surrounding my heart, but I still want to know. So, Lloyd says, he was staying in a hotel there ("Who paid for it?" is my instinctive question, but I keep my mouth shut) and one evening he went downstairs to the pool. There was just one guy swimming there, in his early 40s, handsome, fit, but Lloyd didn't want to swim and went straight into the steam room. Seconds later, the handsome, fit 40-year-old also walked in and sat opposite him. The man then proceeded to open his towel and sit there with what Lloyd describes as one of the biggest dicks he's ever seen.

"It was like a baby's arm, I'm telling you."

Right at this point I'm hyperventilating from jealousy, but I want to hear the rest.

"What happened then?" I ask

"He started stroking it and staring at me."

"And then what?"

"Then I'm not telling you."

"You went and sat on it, didn't you? You slut", I helpfully offer.

"You're calling me a slut? You've had sex with two hundred people."

"Yes, but I'm not a fucking hypocrite about it."

Then Lloyd tells me off for swearing again, but I stay on topic and inform him that I'm adding this person, the sauna guy, to the list of people he's had sex with in the last year, and yes I have been keeping count ever since he told me about his supposed intimacy issues and alleged "sex wall". We are now at three confirmed fucks (all of which I helpfully remind him one by one by repeating stories he's inadvertently told me in the last couple of weeks because he can't keep track of his own lies) and now one tentative fuck that I will corroborate sooner or later.

He tells me I'm insane and leaves the steam room.

On the drive back home, and because I cannot think of anything else right now apart from how many people this man might have had sex with, how frequently, in what positions, and why he won't have sex with me, I decide to ask him about the time that Daniel, Rus, and X flew him out to LA.

"You were here for four days", I say. "How many times did you guys fuck in that time?"

He refuses to answer. I step on the brake and bring the car to a halt in the middle of the road. There is no traffic around us, but there are cars coming up behind in the distance.

"Are you crazy?" he says.

"Yes. I'm not moving until you answer my question."

"I don't know...ten maybe."

I start the car again, because we did make a deal, but I'm focusing on anything but the driving.

"You had sex ten times in three and a half fucking days?" I scream at him.

"Well, there were three of them."

I want to drive into the nearest wall, but that's not guaranteed to kill me, plus I'm getting hard and I want to hear more details.

I violently spit out a number of questions:

"So they took turns on you? Did you fuck and get fucked by each of them? Who has the biggest dick? How soon after they picked you up at the airport did you first fuck? If you got there Friday afternoon and left Monday morning and had sex ten times, that means three times per day on average. When did they all happen?"

He doesn't answer any of my questions, tells me that I'm insane a few more times, adds that I'm not allowed to ask any questions about his previous sex life ever again and then we get home. I go to the bathroom to jerk off again and he sits in the living room to watch TV.

30

For New Year's Eve there is no particular plan, as LA people tend to leave LA and go spend New Year somewhere else. Plus we don't really know any people in LA anyway, so it's not like we'd be invited anywhere even by the few that have stayed here. My suggestion is that we go to this big club downtown, but Lloyd dismisses it as being "a circuit party" and as we all know he doesn't do circuit parties because he's not a typical gay.

By 8pm we have spent the entire day saying to each other, "I don't care what we do, as long as we're together", and one of us even means it. Another suggestion of mine, to walk down to Santa Monica Pier and see what they have going on there, is also dismissed, so around 9pm we end up going online and buying tickets for the club night downtown. I pay the $350 for both of them since it was my idea apparently, plus he doesn't even have money to buy food, let alone nearly 200 bucks to throw away on a gay circuit party, man.

We get to the club around 11pm and the club is really, really packed. Unable-to-move level of packed. I buy us drinks and we walk around the periphery of the dancefloor trying to find some pills to buy. This is particularly important to me, because I am living in blind faith that if Lloyd is high enough he might allow me to have sex with him when we go back home, and yes, I suppose I'll just never learn.

Within the first twenty minutes of being there, it becomes apparent that I'll be spending a very big part of the evening by myself or at best talking to strangers, because Lloyd has decided to put his favourite adage into practice again, one which he exclaimed to me in the first few days after he moved to LA "to be with me", whereby "a good couple is a couple that walks into a party together, they separate, socialise and have a good time individually without being needy, then come together again at the end of the evening and leave".

So I find us some pills, buy us some more drinks and very shortly after I find myself standing alone, trying to find somebody to talk to, even though I am still madly infatuated by the guy who is posing as my boyfriend and living in my house, but wants to have nothing to do with me in both public or intimate situations.

Right before midnight, I make a very concentrated effort to go find him, so that at least we spend the few minutes that will take us into 2014 together. The club has three floors and a few thousand people in it, but I have nothing else to do and I'm very patient, so eventually I run into him. He's hanging out with a group of people he knows who live in New York, apparently, and visiting LA for New Year's. Because I'm very obsessive and quite single-minded and, again, I have very little to do with my life, I recognise one of the New York people as someone that Lloyd has spent a lot of time over the last few months that we've known each other liking Facebook pictures of. He is one of his thousands of Facebook friends and his perfect type, and I suppose that he might have moved to New York to live with him instead if the guy had offered, but I was lucky enough to get in there first.

I'm not the most welcome person to turn up in the group right now, I can tell, and even though Lloyd does me the favour of standing next to me at midnight, he doesn't really want to interact with me and, in fact, cuts me off every time I try to say something to him, complaining that the music is too loud and he can't hear me, so we might as well not speak. A few minutes after midnight, he walks away again.

I spend the next hour by myself. In an unexpected turn of events, Lloyd then shows up complaining that he's been looking everywhere for me and says that I keep disappearing. He asks me for some cash to buy some drinks. I ask whether that's the only reason why he wanted to come find me and he becomes really offended, says, "bub, don't even say that, you know I wanna hang out with you", takes the money and says he's going to the bathroom and will be right back.

The next time that I see him is half an hour later when I'm standing on a balcony on the second floor, overlooking the dancefloor downstairs. I spot Lloyd in the middle of the crowd, standing face-to-face with the Facebook guy from New York. People around them are dancing, walking around, talking, but they're against each other staring into each other's eyes. My heart drops. I stand there staring at them from upstairs, in the distance. I start praying that they don't kiss. They kiss. It lasts for about two minutes, then they pull away and Lloyd looks around, scanning the room, possibly for me. There is no way he can see me where I am. He turns to New York again and nods to him to follow him. I watch them both make their way through the crowd and leave the dancefloor. I can no longer see them now, because they have walked away underneath the balcony where I'm standing.

When we leave the club a couple of hours later, Lloyd is very, very high and I suspect he has taken more pills from other people, or indeed we might have taken the same amount of drugs, but they stopped working on me after a while for obvious reasons. His high is making him extremely arrogant right now and he starts a conversation outside the club (where he wanted to stay longer) about how attractive he is, how everyone finds him desirable, and suggesting we have a competition if I like to see which one of the two of us would be chosen as the hottest. The sad thing is that he's right.

We go home and I get into bed. He goes to the bathroom leaving his phone on the floor next to the bed, which is the biggest indicator of how out of it he really is, because it's usually always attached to his hand and nobody is allowed to touch it. While he's away, the phone keeps buzzing. The phone is locked and he has chosen the setting where the text messages arrive and pop up at the top of the screen but you can't read the first line on a locked screen, you can just see the name of the person texting you. I pick it up and look at it and see the name of the New York guy show up again and again and again.

Lloyd comes back from the bathroom and I tell him he's been getting a lot of text messages. He grabs his phone and reads them. I ask him to tell me who's texting him at 4am and he says that his best friend in Buffalo is drunk and missing him. I ignore his lie plus the fact that I saw him make out with a random guy at the club because I'm scared he'll get mad at me if I say anything and use it as an excuse not to have sex with me and I make a really pitiful attempt to make out with him. He tells me that I can forget it, he's had a shitty night and he's not in the mood, puts a pillow between us and turns around to sleep. None of this has a detrimental effect to how much I want him.

JANUARY 2014

31

Today is my birthday. Some people take the opportunity on their birthday to reflect, think on very self-contained solipsistic level, and become depressed about the passing of time and not having achieved everything they wanted to achieve in their lives yet. I do all those things on any regular day, so today is not going to be that special. The only thing that might be different today is that Lloyd might allow me to touch him sexually, or so he has been promising to me ever since he moved here and it became apparent that we were not going to have a sex life unless some major disruption happened to the space and time continuum, like the earth being sucked into a black hole, my birthday, or him suddenly deciding to be honest for once and telling me why he refuses to have sex with his boyfriend, but will happily do it with other people without giving it a second thought.

I mean, I know the answer of course; I'm not that much of a fool. This is a guy who's not into me at all and is just using me for the time being and in recent weeks I've become painfully aware of this, but until he decides to man up and tell me the truth I might as well keep trying so that I can at least get some return for all the money I'm spending on him.

My happiest day of the year starts off promisingly. Lloyd gives me my present (two pairs of Sperrys that I loaned him money last week to go buy and are in the wrong colour but that's OK, because I can go change them later) and a birthday card that reads:

"I've been thinking and want to tell you I haven't been this happy in my life. You make me the happiest person. Being around you, learning you, experiencing life with you just makes me so beyond content. The ups far outway *[sic]* the downs and the more I get to understand this super complex person, the more I love him. Happy birthday bub. Love, Lloyd."

Then things continue a bit less promisingly, because Lloyd announces that he won't be able to join my birthday dinner this evening, as his best friend from back home is in LA for one evening only on a stopover in his road trip from San Francisco to San Diego and he's promised that he would go see him. I don't ask whether that's the same best friend who was texting him drunk in the middle of the night from Buffalo just yesterday, because I fear that he might get mad at me for uncovering his lies and then break up with me, and he's way too good looking and I don't want that to happen. So I say OK, but can we at least have sex after. He says, "of course we'll have sex on your birthday bub, what are you talking about" and then we go out for a birthday brunch.

Later in the evening I am joined on my birthday dinner by Peter and two of his friends who must have felt sorry for me, and then I go home and patiently wait for my birthday sex to arrive. At around 10pm I call Lloyd to get an update and he answers really, really drunk and slurs that he was just about to drive home, but he realised he's better off waiting to sober up a little first, so right now he's sitting on the pavement right next to his car sipping some water. I'm thinking, finally, this guy has turned around and is a responsible human being, what a dick that I have been for doubting him. At 11.30pm I call again and don't get an answer. At 12.30am, half an hour after my 34th birthday has expired, I stop sobbing hysterically into my pillow, take some Valium and lay in bed awake and brain dead. After 2am, Lloyd comes home. I decide to play it very cool, not ask any questions, and pretend I haven't noticed what time it is.

I've never seen him so drunk in my life. This sounds really dramatic, of course, but I've only been around this person for just over two months. I haven't seen him so drunk in over two months. I'm sure he's gotten a lot more drunk and a lot more frequently, but I just wasn't around. He clearly has no memory of my birthday, my birthday sex, or what year it is. He falls on the bed and launches into an extremely loud story about driving home, then witnessing a car accident, where a maniac who must have been "high on drugs" drove into a barber shop on Santa Monica Boulevard then climbed out of his car screaming with blood on his face and ran away from his vehicle which by that point was on fire while Lloyd stopped driving, waited around and gave an eye witness account to the police when they got there. I nod along for about half an hour while this improbable story is repeated again and again and again with small variations throughout and helpfully exclaim, "oh my god", "are you serious", and "no way" at appropriate points to indicate that I'm listening, very carefully not using any swear words that I know will give him an excuse to get mad at me, then when he's done with repeating the story I make a move to kiss him and he says he just saw a man nearly die, and is sex the only thing I have on my mind? Then I lose all the patience I had collected in the last two months and tell him that I want to break up with him. He says, fine, and falls asleep.

32

On Friday morning, I get up and throw some clothes in a bag. My Dad and his wife are away in Hawaii, so I'm going to go spend the weekend at his house in the Palisades. Unfortunately I'm really weak and very needy and I wait around for Lloyd to wake up before leaving. I want to see what he has to say and whatever it is that he has to say, I want to cling on to it and forgive him and say that I didn't mean it last night and I don't want to break up with him. Then eventually Lloyd wakes up and complains of a headache and asks me if he remembers correctly that I said something about breaking up and I kinda mince my words a little bit and say that, hey, maybe I said something like that but I was really upset because it was my birthday and I'd missed him and I don't *really* want to break up with him, and what does he think?

Then Lloyd tells me that he actually thinks it's a good idea and he's at a very transitional stage in his life where he needs to focus on himself and get his act together and only when he's happy with himself and the way his life is going will he be able to devote himself to another person and be in a good relationship not to mention that he's in a new city and this is all too much for him to take and in summary he is now breaking up with me.

I tell him that I'm going away for a the weekend so we can get a little bit of distance but he can stay at my place and I don't mind, he can take his time moving out, and then he says, before I go away, do I want to go and grab something to eat together and I say, sure, I'd love to do that and somewhere inside I think, oh right, maybe this isn't over yet, he still wants to spend time with me, and suddenly I'm very happy again.

Then we walk to this diner nearby, which I really like because it's so American and quaint and the menu has things like "silver dollar pancakes" and "Aunt Jennie's corned beef hash and eggs" and it's open

24 hours and has a waiter called Doug who's a clear recovering meth addict and has lovely glazed blue eyes that at some point in the past might have even shown signs of life and a bald patch on the crown of his head, and I order some food for myself at the counter and pay, and then Lloyd walks up to me and touches my shoulder affectionately and looks into my eyes and asks, can I get his food as well because right now he has no money at all and I ask, not even money to feed himself, and he says no, and I say that now that he's broken up with me I'm not responsible for feeding him anymore and he gets really mad at me within milliseconds and storms out of the diner and I have to sit there and eat my Idaho rainbow trout burger all alone.

On Friday night I sit by the pool at my Dad's place and don't contact Lloyd at all, but instead I go through his Facebook and look at all his friends and send friend requests to everyone who's male, white, American, aged 18 to 38 and at least a 6 out of 10 in terms of appearance, and there's about 2,000 profiles that fit that description. That boy has a lot of friends and they're all over the country and I'm sure that he doesn't know them, but they must serve a purpose in contributing hundreds of likes every time that he posts something, not to mention the relentless exchange of flirtatious messages and naked as well as semi-naked selfies via inbox. Up to this point and in my whole Facebook career I only added friends that I knew in real life, but where has that gotten me? Single at 34 next to my Dad's pool on a Friday night in January, that's where. While Lloyd's technique of indiscriminate adding (which is how he approached me also initially, lest we forget) has gotten him staying in a beautiful beach apartment in Venice, California for free and having big nights out partying in West Hollywood, again for free. One of us really does have a winning technique.

All these other gay lonely men in need of attention around the country start responding by accepting my friend requests (I have changed my profile picture to a shirtless beach one, strategically) and this appears to have a cumulative effect, as I suddenly also start receiving hundreds of friend requests because I start showing up on people's timelines as having become friends with their friends.

On Saturday daytime I still refrain from contacting Lloyd directly and only around 9pm do I message him and ask how he's doing. He replies about an hour later saying that he's hanging out with his friends in WeHo but it's not going to be a late night, because he doesn't like going out on the scene, as I know. Around 1.30am he gets tagged in a picture at Here Bar on Instagram and between 1.30am and 3am he ignores about 35 calls by me, even though his Whatsapp and Facebook Messenger show to me that he's active on his phone. Eventually he turns his phone off.

On Sunday after 12.30pm he messages me and asks me why I've sent friend requests to all his friends on Facebook and I reply with the question how he was able to go out and get drunk again, if he didn't have money to buy himself some scrambled eggs the day before and I was being asked to pay for his food. He doesn't reply and we don't interact anymore, not even when I get home early on Sunday evening and find him passed out on the couch in the living room.

33

I have never felt as nostalgic for Germany as I do currently, not ever in my life. Ever since I traveled to England when I was 12 and decided that I wanted to be English and then especially from the age of 16 when I actually moved there, I've held Germany in mild disdain. Now I'm constantly watching German TV shows from the '90s on YouTube and listening to German pop songs, again from when I was young, which I had previously turned my nose up at. For the first time in my life also, I am missing my Mum. This has never happened to me before. I guess it took 18 years.

This afternoon I ride my bike to the post office, pick up a postcard, write on it, "Don't think that I never miss you" and send it to her. This will come as a shock, I'm sure, from a child who can never say, "I love you", back every time she says it in my native language, because it feels way too intimate. For that reason alone I phrased my message with two negatives ("don't think", "never miss") so that the end result is a positive message, but not one that you don't have to work around the sentence logically to figure out.

FEBRUARY 2014

34

On Sunday afternoon I am looking for revenge sex on Grindr. Also, not just revenge sex, but anyone to talk to really.

Imagine feeling really down. Imagine having come out of a long-term relationship in a way that really hurt you and being really depressed, so depressed that you can't get it up to go and have sex with anyone else. Then imagine a few months later meeting a new guy that you think you really like and starting to go out with him, but then realising that this new guy is not really into you at all and he's just using you for his own personal reasons. And imagine now not having had sex with anyone in a very long time and feeling very unloved and quite lonely and generally trying to find any answers as to what you've been doing wrong. You will probably be really quite unhappy.

Then on this Sunday afternoon, the guy you were just dating and who's still staying at your house and refused to sleep with you throughout your "relationship" for reasons that he will never explain and you will never understand, the same guy who flipped out on you the first time that you met because you admitted to having used dating apps in the past, does not recognise your headless torso picture because he's an idiot and he sends you a message on Grindr, the app that he has previously refused ever using because it's disgusting to him, and the message says:

"whats up"

Lloyd also has a headless torso on his profile, but I guess I'm not retarded plus I can clearly see my bathroom in the background of the picture where he took it, so I know that it's him. And I write back:

"nm, you?"

I'm at home and he's somewhere that I don't know, but it's 6 miles away according to Grindr. By the time that I've seen his message and written back he's gone offline, so he doesn't reply. At this point I take four Xanax and go for a walk down on the beach.

I come home in the evening and have dinner. Lloyd is still out. I watch some TV in the living room and eventually go into my bedroom to go to sleep. Around half past midnight I hear him come in. He uses the bathroom and from what I can hear goes and lies on the sofa to sleep. I grab my phone and put Grindr on. He's online and he's messaged me back. He still hasn't figured out that it's me.

He says that he likes my picture and asks for some more. I freak out a little bit because I want to keep talking to him to figure out what he wants, how far he would take it with a stranger on Grindr, so I can't tell him that he's talking to me yet. I quickly go on Facebook and steal the pictures of some gay guy I know in London, whose body is similar to mine. All gym gays look the same, after all. I send Lloyd pictures of the London guy and Lloyd sends me back some of himself. I ask him, "What do you like to do" and he replies, "Not a gay club guy. Sports, beach, rock climb, raft, surf, travel, friends, sleep". I try to steer the conversation towards sex. He tells me that he "literally loves fucking and getting fucked". I say that he seems to be pretty close and ask whether he wants to meet now. He finally starts getting suspicious and asks me exactly where I am. I give him an address that's three blocks away. He points out that I seem to be the closest person to him according to the app and doesn't believe me. A couple of minutes later, he blocks me. He has gone back to double-check my profile picture and has now realised it was me all along.

I storm out of my bedroom room and we shout at each other for a bit. I tell him that he's a hypocrite and a liar and he calls me a creep, trying to trick him by messaging him using a fake profile and fake pictures. I remind him that he messaged me first without recognising me, like a moron, and ask him to move out of my place first thing tomorrow. He says that he'll move out when he has the money to do so and tells me that I'm fucking crazy and I should leave him alone, and then I go back to bed and snort three Zopiclone before passing out.

The pills must really have worked, because the next morning I wake up at 11.30am. Lloyd is still lying on the couch. I go sit at the computer and check Facebook to see whom he's added and what pictures he's liked, but realise that he's removed me and blocked me from his friends.

I turn around to face him and ask him if he's fucking kidding me. He scrunches up his face because I used a "cuss word" and I'm therefore immoral and says that, yes, he deleted me and he doesn't want to have anything to do with me anymore. I remind him that he's still living in my apartment for free and that I'm paying for all his food.

We continue arguing and it quickly escalates. The main point of my arguing is that he's an unemployable loser and he needs to get the hell out of my space. The main point of his arguing is that I'm a psychopathic stalker who's obsessed with him. In essence, we are both making extremely valid points, but neither of us is willing to concede that right now.

I am getting more and more aggravated and he's playing it quite cool, but that's mainly because I have feelings for him and he doesn't care about me at all. It's very easy not to lose your temper if you're emotionally uninvolved.

At one point, as I'm shouting at him repeatedly to get out of my house, he takes his phone out and starts recording our argument. I ask him what he's doing and he says that I'm being really hilarious and he wants to play back the argument later to his friends, so they can all see how crazy I am.

I leap forward and try to grab his phone and stop him from recording. He pulls back. As we both scramble for the phone, we fall on the floor and start screaming and punching each other. Somebody starts knocking on my front door and I get up to answer it. The building manager is here to tell me that the neighbours are complaining about the noise. "Can you settle down?" has asks. He doesn't want to have to call the police. I apologise and say that we'll stop right now.

I go back in the living room and continue arguing with Lloyd, only in a quieter voice and sitting down on the sofa. This lasts about fifteen seconds before we start shouting again. This time I take my phone out and call Peter while holding it up in the air. Lloyd asks me what I think I'm doing. I say that if he wants to have evidence of our fight, so do I. I can't quite hear what's happening on my phone, because we're both too loud and I'm not holding it next to my ear, but at this point either

Peter has answered and is listening trying to figure out what's going on, or it has gone to voicemail and it's recording. Lloyd doesn't make an effort to grab my phone or stop me from recording like I did. Instead, he starts yelling that I should step back from him and leave him alone and that I'm really scaring him right now. I'm quite startled because this doesn't make sense, we're both sitting down, and all I can do is ask him what he's talking about, quite incredulously, and point out that I couldn't intimidate him physically anyway because he's much taller than me and weighs 50lbs more. He then shouts, "Put the knife down" (there is no knife, clearly) and I don't even know what's happening anymore, but I think he's just won.

35

Yesterday evening, three months after he moved in, two months after we broke up, and almost three weeks after our physical fight, Lloyd finally moved out of my flat.

I wake up early on Thursday morning to use the bathroom and this is the first time in two months when I don't have to glance over at the living room sofa to check that he's sleeping there, because I know that he's not. Well, it's the first morning when I know for a fact that he won't be there, there's no need to check, and no anxiety comes with the fact that he's not (I used to get very anxious, for example, realising he had gone out and stayed out all night and not come home). But I glance anyway. I go back to bed and take some more Ambien and some more Valium and start checking my phone for messages from different time zones. I think I fall asleep maybe a couple of hours later and wake up after 10am, when I decide to get up.

I have nothing to do today apart from pack for my trip to Hawaii tomorrow morning.

I have breakfast – cereal in a blue bowl and a protein shake from a shaker, both of which we had bought together. As he only moved out yesterday and as we have only lived in this apartment together and have acquired everything in it together, everything reminds me of him now that he's not here.

I decide to do some laundry, primarily for my trip, but also so I can wash the blanket that he used to sleep in on the sofa. It's a plaid blue and maroon blanket from Ralph Lauren that I bought a couple of years ago in London. I have no idea how a flimsy single blanket felt adequate for this enormously muscular man on a bare sofa for the two months that he slept there after he broke up with me. He packed up all his stuff when he left yesterday but this was my blanket, so it stayed, and it's soaked with his scent.

I pick it up and wrap it all around me. I don't think he'll ever hug me again, but right now he encloses me. I fall on the floor with the blanket still around me and I jerk off in it with his smell pushed against my face picturing fucking him hard on all fours. I then do the laundry, fighting thoughts to keep this blanket unwashed forever.

When I bring it back, I wrap it around me once again and lie on the floor. I take a picture of my head with only my eyes peeking out and post it on Instagram with the Cults' lyric "I knew right then that I'd been abducted".

I set off to go to the gym on my bike even though I'm feeling sick. Halfway through, I give up and return home.

36

On Saturday my main focus is to have sex with anyone on this planet for the first time since I had sex with Brett in London before we broke up over a year ago now (discounting my one sexual encounter with Lloyd in Buffalo, which is so faint in my memory right now that I'm starting to question whether it really happened). I am armed with GHB to get me high and horny and forget all the previous exes I'm moping about and a number of Viagra tablets to assist with my emotionally caused impotence problem. I am not going to leave this flat until I manage to do this.

I'm texting Peter and his advice is that I should change my Grindr profile headline to say, "Straight guy looking NOW", and then add some extra information about how I'm not gay, I have a girlfriend, I need to keep this on the down-low, etc, because that's really sexy to guys right now apparently and people will soon start forming a queue to sleep with me.

I go online, make the suggested edits and talk to several people for a couple of hours until I find someone I like, who's willing to come over. This is somebody I've met before, actually, he's a friend of a friend of a friend of a friend and we went to the same concert once when he was visiting London a couple of years ago. I haven't seen him since and it doesn't seem to remember me. He doesn't live very far from me and says he'll be over in half an hour. I take a dose of G, one Viagra, put a record on, and start pacing around the flat, freaking the hell out.

The man that I'm going to have sex with for the first time in over a year arrives and rings my doorbell. He comes upstairs, I open the door, we exchange two sentences of extremely uncomfortable small talk and then start making out. About ten seconds into this, he pulls away and asks, "What did you say your name was?" I tell him my name and ask for his, even though I already know it. He tells me his name. It would seem that now he suddenly remembers me. He then says, "Oh sorry bud, I forgot to put the parking permit in my car downstairs and I might get a ticket. Let me go do that right now". I ask if he actually needs a parking permit, because I have a spare one to give him, but he says no, he lives in the neighbourhood, so he has one. He says he'll be back in two minutes. He leaves my flat. Twenty minutes later, it becomes obvious that he's never coming back. I check Grindr again and he's blocked me, so I can't message him to ask what the deal is. We never exchanged numbers.

I text Peter with everything that happened. He tells me to take another dose of G and keep trying. I take another dose of G, spend about half an hour talking to more people, then I get really tired most likely because I took too much G and I fall asleep on my sofa. I wake up about an hour later and check my messages. Within an hour, a 22-year-old student who's just moved to LA has been to my place and we have fucked each other. The actual sex must have lasted about six minutes. It was a dreadful experience, but at least I am now sexually active again.

On Friday evening Peter comes over to Venice and we go out to eat. I am feeling particularly down, even by my own recent standards. When dinner is over, we go back home and take a couple of doses of a morphine-based painkiller that Peter has saved from last year when he was prescribed it after dislocating his shoulder. I have this idea that I want to take a bath and I want Peter to be there and watch me, but I don't want him to be able to touch me or be part of it in any other way. Peter agrees to that. I take my clothes off and get in the bath. Peter sits on a chair in the bathroom and watches, and then about twenty minutes later he says that he doesn't want to do this anymore and he goes home.

MARCH 2014

37

On Thursday night I finish some work and then walk down to the beach to watch the sunset by myself and listen to some music, but then hurry back home before the sun has gone down because I remember I need to cut the sleeves off a shirt that I just bought before going to the gym tonight and this is making me lose concentration right now until it's finally and properly done.

At home, while I'm measuring fabric that's about to get cut, I receive a Facebook message from somebody I'm friends with but I don't know how and the message says:

"Sorry for the ambush ass vid. Had some wine and was feeling horny for you lol."

Then he attaches a video of him sitting up on a sofa, spreading his legs and jiggling his ass. It looks good.

I tell him that I saw a picture he posted today and that I thought he looks good, but the video is killing me and he's sexy as fuck. He then tells me that he wants to meet me so bad and asks if I ever go up to Oregon. I say no. We then go back and forth for a bit discussing meeting up for a sex weekend, either in LA or Oregon or somewhere in between, and we exchange a few more pictures and videos.

Then Anthony, whom I've started talking to again, texts me and he says:

"The hottest guys are at Pavillions right now, I am purposely driving around the parkin lot to see what cars they get into. Don't judge."

I write back:

"You are talking to a guy who's going to the gym tonight at 11pm just to work out next to a hot guy who was there last night at the same time, who am I to judge?"

"One just got in a jeep."

"Very good."

Then I send Anthony the original ass video from the guy from Oregon and Anthony asks who that is and I say that it's a random Facebook guy who's drunk and sending me videos and wants to drive to LA to get fucked and Anthony says that well, he's been to Oregon and he's seen what's there, so this makes total sense.

Then he texts me that the other hot guy got in an Audi and that we should go to grocery stores to cruise more often, I agree, cut my shirt ready for the gym, wait around for a couple more hours doing nothing and then set off to catch my gym crush at 11pm.

38

In the evening, I go to the gym. On Thursday nights on my way there I ride my bike past a soup kitchen, where a bunch of people line up to get fed. Sometimes I check them out. Sometimes there are hot ones. Sometimes they are blond. You know there is no god when you see blond homeless people.

At the gym, there is a guy who's been genetically modified by torturous aliens to appeal to sad gay men by being physically perfect. They have also dressed him head to toe in store-window, current season Nike apparel, and have given him a badass Mercedes to drive because they know we're all about the surface. I work out my legs and stare at him for the duration of my workout, walking around with perfect posture, towering over everyone, performing robotically perfect back and shoulder exercises, his muscles bulging from every possible direction, hurting me inside. From his shin hair peeking underneath his calf-length Nike leggings and his square shoulders, to his cutthroat jawline and the stern look in his eyes, he is perfect. I am using all my strength not to run up to him sobbing and beg him to love me, or at least let me lick his sweaty armpit once and forget about me forever. Either will do.

Then I leave the gym and turn on Grindr, just at the off chance that he's gay. The gym robot isn't on it, but some other guy from the gym has messaged me. He is unattractive to me and therefore invisible. The invisible person, whom I genuinely don't remember seeing in the gym at all, has said:

"All the sexy guys at the gym at this time."

I don't want to commit that it was me that he saw yet (my profile has a headless torso picture) so I say:

"They are?? Who's there?"

"Were you at the gym?"

Then I give up, plus I want to talk about the gym robot, so I type:

"Sure I was. Which guys did you like?"

"Any pic?"

"Let's just talk about the other guys"

"Which one did u like", the invisible man asks me.

"I like the tall one with the shaved head who wears full Nike outfits all the time."

"He was wearing blue today huh?"

"Yes. What's his deal?"

"Yes I saw him. He's huge."

"I know. I'm in lust with him. Why does he walk around like that?"

"He knows he's good."

Then I type:

"You have to do something."

Then I type:

"You have to get him for me."

Then I type:

"I can't live like this anymore."

And then the invisible person stops responding to me, so I guess we are through.

39

On Wednesday I start my day successfully by waking up.

Today we are lucky enough that a bro meme appears as soon as I open Facebook and scroll through my timeline. A few pop news websites have picked up a story that appeared on last night's MTV reality show "True Life" about a 22 year old college baseball bro, whose biggest problem in life is his giant butt. A short clip of the show has been reposted around, where he complains that no one takes him seriously. That he goes out and feels objectified. That he's worried his career will suffer (he's graduating this year) because in any office he works in, the ass will be the distraction that will overshadow his achievements. All this is complaining is delightfully interspersed with shots of him going up and down stairs, tearing through pairs of trousers, waddling into college parties, and swinging baseball bats with his, objectively, enormous butt, which was made exclusively to be worshipped by gay men, in primary focus.

All the elements of this story are making me short-circuit. There is an all American athletic bro. He plays college baseball. He is tall, white, blue-eyed, and he has an unnaturally big butt. He is tortured and he needs help. My help. This is all too much. I need to track him down.

I spend a good half hour replaying the short clip from Facebook with the highlights of the show and reading the comments that other desperate gays such as myself have left on the news sites that reported this. I then find the actual show online in MTV and watch it twice. Following that, and now in a complete frenzy because nowhere is there a mention of his surname, we only get a reference to his stupid generic first name ("Jake"), and I can't find him online, I start going mental on google. I google the TV show. I google the state where he lives and his name. I google his sister's first name (who also appeared on the show to provide moral support), in conjunction with his name and the state where they live. Nothing. Then I go back and watch the show a third time and try to find a name for the college that he attends. They are too smart and they haven't given it. Then as I watch his beautiful dumb sad eyes nearly in tears once again because a girl shouted "dat ass" as he walked past her last night, I have an epiphany. He plays baseball, doesn't he? I go on google and search for all the college baseball teams that exist in his state. Do you know how many Jakes play college baseball in Kentucky? Many. But I have plenty of time and all the patience in the world and I finally find him. I now have a few more pictures, his height (6'2"), weight (210lbs), and a lovely little blurb about what he likes to do in his spare time. I look him up on Facebook, Twitter, and Instagram and follow him on all three.

Then it's suddenly late afternoon and I walk to Whole Foods to buy some lunch, because I've forgotten to eat today so far.

APRIL 2014

40

A couple of days ago, I messaged Lloyd on Facebook. I really want to see him again. He took his time but eventually he got back to me and I forced a brief conversation out of him and then asked if he wanted to have dinner some time. He said yes, so I suggested this Friday. We're supposed to meet tonight.

I call him up to set up a time and decide on a place and he even answers on my third attempt (even though I'm also checking his Scruff profile at the same time and he is constantly online there, which means that he's holding his phone in his hand but just deciding to ignore my first couple of calls) and suggests that we go to a sushi place in West Hollywood. I say fine and ask if he wants me to pick him up instead of both of us driving there and trying to find parking and he says, no, he'll drive himself there, thank you very much. I say that this doesn't make sense and I think that he just doesn't want me to know where he lives and he says that damn right he doesn't want me to know where he lives. I ask him why and he says because it's his life and he doesn't want his ex boyfriend to know where he lives. I tell him that this is really offensive and remind him that he stayed at my place for three months for free and he still owes me a lot of cash on top of that if he really needs to hear it, and in any case we are friends now and any normal person wouldn't have a problem telling his friends where he lives. He tells me that he agreed to have dinner tonight at a real push but since I'm acting like this I can forget about it and hangs up on me. This really freaks me out and I call him right back and my eyes are getting wet and he picks up and I apologise for being so irrational as to wanting to know where he lives and say that of course we can meet at the restaurant and we agree to meet at 8pm. We hang up and I already hate both him and myself more than I did half and hour ago and who would have thought this would even be possible.

After this I spend a little bit of time staring at a wall obsessing about my loneliness and thinking what time I should go to the gym, until I receive a poke and an inbox message on Facebook. They are both from a gentleman called Seth Ryder and the message reads:

"I'm not sure what the definition of a poke is, but I did it, and there's no turning back"

Now, I don't know Seth in real life, but it turns out that he follows me on Instagram and he has a very hot boyfriend that I'm definitely very interested in, so I assume that in order to get to the boyfriend, I have to talk to Seth first. Both Seth and his boyfriend appear to live in Chicago. I write back:

"I'm learning about pokes as I go along, just like you, but this was certainly not objectionable. How's it going?"

Then we make some small talk, how the week is treating us, where are we from, what we do, until I finally ask him if he has a boyfriend. Then the following conversation happens.

Seth: "Yes, I do. He's in law school and lives in a different city right now."

Me: "How far is this different city? Long distance can be hard."

Seth: "About 3 hours away. We've got it down though so it's not too bad. And anyway, we may be together but we're not dead. Ha"

Me: "I'm trying to read between the lines in what you just said, but I'm too stupid. Please rephrase?"

Seth: "My bad. I think a lot of people have preconceived notions of what a relationship is or should be and that we operate more under what works for us may not work for everybody. We're together but not dead to the world as individuals."

Me: "I think you're implying that you are free to sleep with other people. Is this correct?"

Seth: "You've seen right through me. This is partially true. There are rare occasions where another person is involved, but that's something we do together."

Me: "Got it. Everything is clear now. You sometimes have threesomes, and you would like me to be part of that."

Seth: "Maybe I should have just come out and said that."

Me: "Said what?"

Seth: "Hi, I'm Seth. I sometimes have 3somes with my boyfriend and we want to have one with you."

Me: "Hi, I'm Konrad. I sometimes take part in 3somes as a third, and I would like to have one with you and your boyfriend."

Seth: "Well I'm glad we got that established. I guess I can give up playing shy and just say flattering things to you."

Me: "You don't have to say flattering things, but you can give up playing shy for sure."

Seth: "Perfect. So what does it take to get my hands on you?"

At this point I screenshot the conversation and send it to Peter, along with the Instagram profile links for Seth and his boyfriend. Then I reply to Seth.

Me: "Well, I suppose distance is one really prohibitive factor at the moment"

Seth: "That's easily taken care of. Just know that I'd really like to. Get my hands on you. Or rather we'd like to."

At this point this is really turning me on because it's such a Lloyd M. scenario: talking to some couple in another city, being flirty as fuck, getting them to fly you out there for a sex weekend. And seeing that Lloyd is my current obsession and I want to emulate everything that he does, well, I'm really into this. So I continue with Seth.

Me: "This sounds very good to me. So am I visiting Chicago?"

Seth: "Yeah! I'm all for that. You're welcome any time."

Then I also screenshot this to Peter and add, "Why is he not offering to fly me out yet", and Peter writes back, "I guess you're good, but not that good", and then I leave the conversation with Seth because I assume I have to play hard to get a little bit at least, and then the flight offer will come in the next few days. (In the next few days, the flight offer does not come).

In the evening when it's time to go meet Lloyd I drive over to WeHo, park, and wait outside the restaurant. He shows up fifteen minutes late despite the place being a few minutes away from his house (I don't know exactly where he lives, but he does live in WeHo) and my drive here having taken nearly an hour, but immediately when I see him I forgive him everything and, in fact, start wondering why he doesn't treat me even more like shit than he currently does, because someone who looks like that should get away with everything and I'm not worthy of him.

During dinner we talk about work a little bit, our families, living in LA, and then he wants to discuss boys and exchange dating stories and all I can think is, you fucking cruel, dumb bastard, can you not see that I'm madly in love with you and every thought of you existing and having a life outside this dinner table right now slices my heart like a knife and the last thing I want to hear is who's been fucking you, so I say that maybe we should just stay clear off such topics for a while, and change the subject. Then we have managed to fall out and stop talking to each other by the end of dinner anyway and I drive back to the beach severely depressed.

41

On Sunday morning I wake up and go to the gym and then the beach and I'm sure I was supposed to also work for a bit because my Dad has been complaining that I'm not putting in as many hours as he would like me to, but suddenly it's 8pm in the evening I've completely run out of time and a masc musc bro from Grindr is about to come over to mine. Yes, this masc musc bro is 6'2" and yes he's studying at the moment and working part-time as a model and yes he's got all the muscles that you want him to have, but primarily the reason why I want it so bad is that his blurb on Grindr is that he refuses to accept messages from anyone who has a visible face on their profile picture because those people are out and shameless and clearly non masc enough, which means that he has gigantic issues about his sexuality, is self-hating to the nth degree and his internalised homophobia might just be surpassing mine. Add to that the fact that some of his messages to me have included, "aight bro", "yo", "right on", "down to wait", "for sure bro", "solid", "I'm horny bro", and "leaving in 10 bro", and I have no choice but to collapse into a heap and meet this guy.

I've never met so many homophobic gay guys as I have since I moved to America. The word "discreet" is by far the most commonly used description in Grindr bios, with the only competition coming from the number of people who state "neg4neg" and type in the date of when they were last tested and found "clean". Effeminate guys who are HIV positive must not get any action at all on this continent. I don't understand why everyone is in the closet. What are all these masculine, grown gay men so afraid of?

Then my guy turns up in a large SUV and I go outside to hand him a permit so he can park on my street. I walk up to his car, he opens his window and I attempt some small talk. He grunts a couple of times and drives off to find a parking spot. I sit down on the steps outside my building to wait for him, and he only comes back around ten minutes later, by which point I have started to think that he took one look at me, changed his mind, and drove off. Also stealing my permit.

But even now, upstairs in my apartment, he's completely masc musc and gives one-word answers and even those are so mumbled to the point where I think that he might be mentally impaired, and he doesn't smile even for a second or show any human emotion that might indicate he wants to be there, and I don't even know that he's into me or completely repulsed and is still trying to make a quick escape, until his tongue is in my mouth and our baseball caps are clashing against each other. Then we have sex, and I can objectively rate this as a 5.4/10 experience, one that was a lot better in my head before he turned up.

Then the awkward time comes when I have to walk him to his car so I can pick up my permit, and those few minutes are spent making stilted conversation where I ask him questions about himself, where he grew up, what he's studying, and he's coming up with lies for each one whilst looking extremely uncomfortable, because, I don't know, I'll track down his parents, run straight to them and tell them that their son is gay? Something like that.

When I get back home, I jerk off and cum once again, because I'm still hard from the Viagra I took to get through this. Then Peter starts texting me drunk from a work colleague's gay wedding where he's gone tonight in a town called Ojai, northwest of Los Angeles.

Peter: "I'm now walking 1.4 miles back to the hotel because there are no cabs here."

Me: "Can't one of the drunk guests drive you?"

Peter: "We were lured to a pool party that never happened."

Me: "Those fucking gays."

Peter: "Exactly!"

Peter: "I got really drunk and told everyone about sleeping with [well known gay singer Peter has slept with]

Me: "That's nice"

Peter: "I then pleaded with everyone to tell me something more shameful."

Peter: "And my boss said he likes to piss on guys."

Me: "You gays kill me."

Peter: "Which of course made me OBSESSED with my boss"

Peter: "I MUST HAVE HIS PISS."

Me: "Ask for a urine sample. Or does it have to stream directly for you to be happy?"

Peter: "I will not be satisfied until my boss pees on me. What happens after that is none of my concern."

Peter: "This is all very real."

Peter: "Should I sleep with my boss?"

Me: "Yeah man, why not?"

Peter: "Orrrr...should I want to sleep with him and become obsessed?"

Me: "The latter. 100% the latter."

Peter: "Really????? I grabbed his back sexually several times."

Me: "Yeah really. Imagine the drama, the intrigue, the plotting, the heightened emotions."

Peter: "Fine. He now knows that another daddy fucked me repeatedly and I know that he pissed on guys several times. But we will just go on with our business as usual."

Me: "That's better than doing anything with him. If you do anything with him, it will become boring. This is intense."

Peter: "That's true. Thank you."

Then this conversation ends and I decide to text the closeted guy from earlier and tell him that I had a really good time, not because I actually did, but because I want him to respond and say the same thing to me, because I can't stand knowing that he possibly didn't like me, so I write:

"That was fun, dude."

He writes back, "It was for sure", one hour and ten minutes later, which indicates that he doesn't think it was fun at all either, and then I go to bed.

42

On Thursday morning I wake up and I'm reading the news, because I thought of this new concept where sometimes you have to be less insular and self-absorbed and maybe look at the world around you and realise that other people have problems too and you're not the centre of the fucking universe. I guess it's worth trying.

I'm reading news from Europe, and particularly this story that broke in Greece last week about a kid in some small town up north, who went missing about a month ago. He was 20. So he went missing and they were trying to find him for several weeks, and the things that came out while they were trying to find him were that he used to be bullied really badly and the code words that were used for the reasons why he was bullied were that he "wasn't masculine enough" and he was "too quiet" and he didn't live up to the "manly" ideals that a 20-year-old guy should live up to, behaviourally. Then last week he was found dead. At the point when I'm writing this it's not yet known whether someone killed him or whether he killed himself, but I believe the narrative doesn't change that much either way.

So when they found this kid dead, there was an uproar in Greece and everyone stood by his side on TV and on the internet, which are the places that matter now, in our century, and of course there were some oddball idiots who wrote things against him still, but they were just a small minority that was quickly dismissed. And everyone's uproar concerned "bullying", a word which is now used in its English form in Greek because there's no Greek equivalent, or so these articles tell me, and everyone was up in arms about this phenomenon and wanted it to stop. Right now. The fact that the kid was implied to be gay and that's why he was bullied is not something that's said out loud, because even now, with incidents like this, it's not something that can be brought up explicitly in some societies, and even the biggest supporters of Vangelis, because that's the kid's name, are not fighting a fight for gay acceptance, they are fighting a fight for those men who are "not masculine enough", or "too quiet". But it's fine. Societies advance at their own pace and for now in Greece they're going to have to use codes.

And this story kinda hurt me when I read about it, because hey, I was that quiet kid in Germany once that was bullied to the point where I had to change schools and I therefore now still begrudge Germany a little bit because my brain may be able to process things in a more advanced way, but my soul works on a more linear level, which I haven't been able to develop yet, I'm sorry. So anyway, I caught glance of this story and then I kept clicking through and reading more and more articles and views and message boards and comments sections and it didn't get any less hurtful and I kinda loathe people who claim that reading stuff on the internet brought them to tears, so I'll leave this here.

And then, with all that, I thought, well, what the hell am I doing as a grown, out gay man spending all my time pretending to be straight with all my baseball caps and basketball shorts, especially now that I'm living in America. How am I helping anyone to feel comfortable with themselves, if they're insecure, if they're not out, and what is the message that I'm giving out. Are they only going to be accepted, is their only hope to stay alive, first literally and then metaphorically, in a grown up society if they're acting more straight than the straight dudes?

I think about masculinity a lot and what it means and how it's qualified against being a homosexual male. The truth is that I'm not comfortable around really effeminate gay men who squeal and cackle and prance. But the truth also is that I'm not comfortable around really masculine straight guys who yell and growl and shout at sports on TV. I think this happens because I'm quiet and introverted and those groups are both loud and extroverted and I feel they suck out my energy when I'm around them. I don't want the effeminate gay guys to act more masculine though, that's not my problem.

Now, in any case, masculinity is a big thing even outside the small towns of northern Greece. You may not be bullied explicitly for not being masculine in West Hollywood in LA and in Soho in London, but the predominant behavioural ideal right now is heteronormative. Via Sean Cody. And yes, I exclusively use porn sites to study and determine social norms. Heteronormative males are what the majority of us jerk off to and what the majority of us want to be. I think it's a little awful, that this is the principal ideal.

Not to mention, this obsession with masculinity and the dismissal of any alternative sips into the slang used by gay males. We often use female pronouns to talk dismissively about others when we want to degrade them, or even gently mock them. When you're mad at your friend and you text your other friend and say, "She's a bit crazy, that one", you attempt to diminish them by taking away their masculinity. I think it's all connected. I may be mad.

Then there is the go-to gay slur from one gay male to another, of course, about being a bottom. Everyone is always fucking accused of being a bottom. Nobody uses the term "top" dismissively. Nobody leaves anonymous comments on websites accusing people of being tops. This takes us full circle, back to cultures where being a bottom equals being gay, but being a top means that you're just a guy who likes to fuck.

Anyway, why does the world think like that? Why are effeminate men berated? Actually, why are women still perceived as less equal? Is this gay issue ultimately a sexism issue? I don't get it. I don't know what to do. As an out gay man, I don't want young kids who are not out to be scared. I certainly don't want them to get bullied and disappear and kill themselves. But I also don't want them to think that they can only fit in by acting the way society tells them to.

MAY 2014

43

On Monday morning I wake up and possibly do some work or other activities or breathe or allow my heart to circulate blood around my body, but it's rather unclear, because there's only one purpose to the day, one thing that I'm avoiding thinking about, because it's the only thing I can think of: Lloyd has agreed to meet up with me later this afternoon, because I've got something very important to tell him. Everything is relative, of course, and I don't think that anything that can come out of my mouth at this stage would be classified as "important" by Lloyd, but I suppose I'm judging this by my own pathetic standards.

I hold back from texting him to set the time for our meeting until 2pm, at which point I finally break and send him a message.

"What time can you meet?"

He leaves me hanging for an hour and then he replies:

"Can't meet afterall, wrkng through my break"

I write back asking whether he has ten minutes to spare and that I can drive to him myself, if I have to, then I send two more texts telling him that this is "really, really, really, really important" and he texts back:

"Yes"

We agree to meet at a coffee shop near where he works for a few minutes in an hour.

Lloyd and I broke up four months ago now or were never together, depending on what one's definition of a relationship is. After not talking at all for a month and a half, we met up and hung out a couple of times, which could be described as anything from disastrous to civil, but nothing further up the positive end of the scale. In my heart there's hope for a reunion. My brain, however, says that my heart is a fucking idiot.

I arrive at the coffee shop and sit there with a bottle of water, a copy of *The Sun Also Rises*, and my phone showing a note, where I've written down what I want to say.

Lloyd shows up and sits opposite me. For the first time I accept the fact that his eyes are green and not blue like I've always wanted them to be. Perhaps this is a defence mechanism for what's about to happen and I've already started protecting myself. (Surely getting turned down for the third time by somebody with green eyes is going to destroy me less than somebody blue-eyed).

Lloyd makes casual conversation for about ten minutes and of course that's very easy for him, because this meeting doesn't hold the same life-threatening importance that it's holding for me.

Once he's done, I deliver my speech almost straight from my phone's notes, a speech, which goes something along these lines (oh, OK, verbatim these lines):

"I know you don't want to have a serious talk, but I need to get this off my chest. It's been clear from the last few months that you're not in love with me. You don't have romantic feelings for me. But I have these feelings for you. And that's fine. But I need to look out for myself. I need to know. Tell me that you don't have any feelings for me. Tell me that you don't now, and that you never will. I need you to set me free. Let me off the hook, so I can move on."

Then Lloyd sets me free.

He leaves the coffee shop in a huff when I ask him, please, not to contact me in any way for the foreseeable future and I also get up and go seconds later to avoid the stare from the middle aged writer at the next table who has overheard the entire conversation.

I drive back home, where I don't feel anything for approximately four hours.

Then I go to the gym. I am stupid enough to go to the gym where I used to go when Lloyd wasn't living in LA yet, and we had a completely fictitious, perfect, long-distance relationship. I haven't been to that gym since he moved here. The fact that I'm there now, trying to relive all the memories of how things were before reality hit and it all went sour, is surely a demonstration of my emotional masochism.

I sit at the bench where I used to do shoulder press all those months ago when I went to the gym late in the evening, so that I could text Lloyd when he was in bed, right before he would go to sleep. I start missing everything that we think we had. I start missing the plans that we made, the promises to each other, and our dreams for our life together. I start missing my own stupid ideas of going to this gym with him, seeing him in the distance and feeling proud that he's mine, my stupid ideas of having a family, two boys and a girl, our fights about what they should do with the spare time – I want them to read, he wants them to play sport – and how we'd spend our holidays sometimes in Berlin, visiting my family, and sometimes in Buffalo, visiting his. My stupid ideas of a life shared, based on nothing but my pure loneliness and all the different ways in which I'm fucked up and will forever be.

I walk to the locker room to continue bawling my eyes out in one of the bathroom stalls, where I try unsuccessfully to drown my sobs in some toilet tissue, until I decide that I've embarrassed myself enough and I leave the gym.

On the drive back home, I continue to cry, because I'm now seriously self-harming by playing a playlist with songs that remind me of him, purposefully compiled last week. A black Mercedes stops next to me at the traffic lights and the driver – young white male, possibly late 20s – glances over at me, sees that I'm sobbing and continues to stare.

44

My next-door neighbour, Elvira, is a middle aged lady that has modeled her life on the mannerisms and general demeanour of Diane Keaton, only with even more of that contrived, stammering ditziness, if that's humanly possible, and with the added toll that several decades of living in a small, rent-controlled, beach apartment while watching life pass you by, have taken. I'd never even seen her during the first few months of living here, although, in retrospect, our first indirect interaction came early on when she alerted the building management during a fight with Lloyd. There was no one else in the building that could have done it. It was a weekday, in the middle of the day, and I believe the majority of the other residents have jobs. Not to mention that much later, once she had launched her friendliness attack on me and we were talking regularly (needless to say, against my will) she once came up to me and asked me "if I have a cold because she can hear me sneezing a lot" so she keeps pretty close track of what goes on in my apartment. Fights with boyfriends, sneezing, clipping nails, she keeps a tab on everything.

So once she came over and introduced herself a couple of months ago, the floodgates of intrusiveness opened. What was previously quiet espionage was now explicit surveillance. I certainly don't think I'm special to her in those terms, I'm pretty sure she keeps an eye on everyone in the building, it's just that I make it particularly easy for her by living right next-door. If I play along to this close relationship that she wants us to have, it's all fine. Please note, based on her suggestions over the time we've known each other, the close relationship that she wants us to have includes keeping our front doors open so the other person come in and out and chat at their will, getting high together on evenings when we're bored, and giving the other person a key to our apartment every time we go away for the weekend "for emergencies". When I don't play along and try to maintain some privacy or establish some barriers, I see the other, non-hippy side of her.

One of her most unfortunate habits (unfortunate for me) is that she loves to stand outside my kitchen window and talk to me while I make food, wash dishes, or whatever. I mean, I find this to be almost a criminal violation. One time, she was walking past my window as I was walking away and we caught glimpse of each other. Because it all happened too quickly and we didn't have the chance to talk to each other, she stopped walking, put her hands on either side of her face to shield away any reflections on the glass and stuck her nose to the outside of my window, so she could follow me around and see where I was going inside my apartment. This was a bit too much, and even as insipid and socially inept as I am, I decided to complain to her. Then, I kept the kitchen window curtains closed for a few days just to drive the point home. During those days, each time she saw me coming in or out of my apartment she refused to acknowledge me at all. At the end of the week, and as I was leaving, she heard me, burst out of her apartment and told me that everyone in the building hates me because I bang my front door every time I come in or out, and would I mind being a bit more quiet, thank you very much. The next day I opened my curtains again, because I didn't want the grief. Our friendship was reinstated immediately after that.

The problem with all this, sadly, is that my neighbour is just the female version of me in twenty-five years. During our frequent one-sided catch-ups, she has often shared stories of her youth, referring to herself as a former "beach babe", mentioning surfing adventures, carefree trips along the California coast, and flings with men who ended up being wrong for her. Please tell me that this isn't me. Please give me a guarantee that I won't be here, living in this same apartment at 58, unemployed, aimless, and insane, occupying myself with peeking through my neighbours' windows, trying to live vicariously through them. So sometimes, for extremely selfish reasons and in the hope that in the future when I am Elvira my young neighbours will do the same for me, I think that I should probably humour her, be friendly, and give her some attention. Other times, and despite my occasional good intentions, she makes this very difficult.

On this Wednesday evening, I'm home alone and trying to pull myself away from refreshing Facebook and go to bed. It's minutes before midnight.

I hear a knock on the door, and of course I know it's Elvira and I seriously consider not answering, but she knocks again, more fervently this time, and I know this is just not going to go away.

I open the door and she storms in holding a candlestick. I am not making any of this up. She's sorry she had to bother me, she says, unclear whether she's more or less sorry compared to the other five times she did in the last couple of weeks with an urgent story of low-stake apartment building warfare somehow connected to her self-assigned role as neighbourhood watch official, but something really disturbing is happening and she needs my help.

I almost say, "what is it", but in reality this is not a discussion where my input is needed, she can continue the dialogue for both of us just taking minor cues from my facial expressions or stance: half a raised eyebrow here, a minor shift of my eyeballs there, blinking, shifting the weight between my legs as I stand there otherwise inanimate, it all counts as my part of the conversation.

This time she tells me that she's heard some noises and wants me to go investigate the apartment downstairs from hers, because she thinks someone is getting murdered very quietly, or having violent sex very quietly, both of which she thinks she can help with. I say no. She says, fine, if she goes downstairs and someone is getting murdered and she gets caught up herself I will have it on my conscience, and my silence must indicate that I'm fine with that, because she leaves, candlestick in hand and heads down the corridor.

I listen out for approximately two seconds and still I hear nothing, and then log on to RealJock, where some guy, 24, from San Diego, with the username cherishme1 has written:

"hey, hows u? you're gorgeous, just had 2 say! lol. the gf thinks you're hot 2 x"

I click on his profile and he's not attractive to me, also this whole thing is completely fake and ridiculous, of course, so I write back immediately:

"Thanxs. Can I watch you fuck your girlfriend, then fuck you"

Him: "you're welcome :D so whats up? u bi or gay? im bi n she knows lol. u work out? looks like u do, I do. sure haha x"

Me: "Gay. sometimes I workout. Where do you live? Show me yr body"

Him: "nice lol. since u seen me, wanna c a pic of the gf? maybe gay but can still judge haha. attached pic x"

I say, sure, I'd love to see a picture of your made up girlfriend (only I withhold the "made up"), he sends a picture of some girl, tells me she has 34DD tits and then asks if he can ask a question. I say, ask.

He then writes, "even though you're gay, would u ever make an exception? with her x", and this has gotten more boring even than going and investigating quiet murders with my crazy neighbour, so I shut everything down and go to bed.

45

On Tuesday I aim to get up really early and go get my haircut, because the later you go, the longer you have to wait. I manage to wake up and make it to the barbershop at 10.30am, which is not early, not early at all, and there about eight people ahead of me. Potentially you can call up in advance and make an appointment, but the time has not come yet when I'm prepared to make a phone call and talk to somebody that's not immediate family or current boyfriend, so that's just not going to happen.

I used to cut my own hair between the years 2005 and 2014, but then I was suddenly 34 and I lost my youth and could use all the help I could get, so I decided to have it done by someone who knows what they're doing. Well. $25-worth knows that they're doing. I certainly don't want to be one of those gays with the fancy $80 haircuts, who also get a neck trim every week between haircuts so it always looks immaculately groomed and pristine at all times, because then you're suddenly a fashion gay and nobody likes those at the moment. Well, I don't. So I have my hair cut one week, then it looks good for a week or ten days after that and then it starts looking awful, so I start wearing a hat constantly for three weeks, and then I have my haircut again.

My barbershop is run by a group of no-nonsense straight Latino bros, and I'm afraid I don't know enough about this demographic first-hand to write about it in a derogatory manner, like I do with white bros, scene gays, or troubled ex-pats running away from themselves. I do know that they talk endlessly about baseball, breasts and other blue-collar topics that I don't understand. The person who cuts my hair is my favourite, because he never attempts to start a conversation with me. I suspect that's because he knows I'm foreign and don't follow the Dodgers, and what the hell would he have to talk to me about? He's also my favourite because he's quiet overall, compared to the others. I also like going there because I'm an ethnic minority and it always feels like the beginning of those porn scenes where a clueless white guy walks into a garage full of tattooed, ethnically-diverse meatheads after his car has broken down in the middle of the desert and they proceed to gang rape him, not that I want this to actually play through, as in real life I refuse to engage sexually with anyone unless they have blue eyes or lighter and an Anglo-Saxon surname that goes back at least five generations.

This Tuesday morning the barbershop TV is playing the 1977 bodybuilding documentary *Pumping Iron*, starring Arnold Schwarzenegger. The gumball candy machine they keep near the entrance next to the jar full of pennies is empty (who eats those, I wonder). And they have finally moved the naked pin-up calendar hanging on the wall from the month of February (where it was all through February, March, and April) to November, arbitrarily. Maybe there weren't any hot girls during the spring and summer months. The most important conversation that takes place is the following:

Young Latino customer: "I need to have my hair cut because I'm going to a wedding"

Head barber: "Oh yeah? Who you going with?"

Customer: "On my own probably"

Head barber: "But who are you leaving with?"

Customer: "The baddest one there"

Head barber: So you want the 'going to a wedding on my own, but leaving with the baddest one there' haircut?"

Customer: "Yessir"

Head barber: "Dis what I do"

Mateo finishes my haircut, gives me a voucher for three free boxing classes, which I take both as a compliment and an insult, I pay him and leave.

From there I drive to Beverly Hills to have an MRI scan on my wrist, which has been hurting me for four weeks now ever since I fell off my bike and landed on it. I went to the hospital as soon as it happened and had an x ray and it wasn't broken and I've been wearing a brace to support it since, but the pain hasn't gone away, and obviously

I couldn't give it a rest and stop working out, because what would I be without the gym, the source of all of my confidence and my only social outlet most days, but here I am a month later, still in pain, so I have to have it checked out.

I check in with Maria and Brittany in reception and they take me to a room, where I can put all my stuff in a locker and wait. Then Jimmy the MRI technician comes in and tells me that it won't be much longer now, maybe eight more minutes and I'm fine with that to be honest, and then suddenly Jimmy asks me if I'm going to the game later and it takes two seconds of him pointing at my head for me to remember that I put on an LA Dodgers cap that I found in my car after my haircut because I didn't want small hairs to keep falling on my face and neck. I laugh awkwardly and say, no, but it's already too late and Jimmy has taken me for a big sports fan and is now talking about a conflicting schedule this evening with the Lakers. I'm thinking, honestly, Jimmy, can you not hear me speak? What Dodgers? What Lakers? What are you talking about?

Then Jimmy goes away and what might have been a nice, boring eight-minute lull with me watching CNN news on the small TV near the ceiling and flicking through half-year-old copies of People magazine, has now become an agonising countdown before Jimmy returns with more incomprehensible SportsCenter talk that I will have to navigate.

The terror of Jimmy returns in eleven minutes and twenty-three seconds, yes, I set the stopwatch on my phone after he left to count the sweet minutes of loneliness, and takes me to the next room where he has to do some paperwork about my case and ask me the very important question:

"So is baseball your favourite sport then?"

Then I mumble something about soccer and being European and that sets him off on a very fervent dialogue (monologue) about the World Cup and all the different countries that prefer different sports and about sports video games and the most popular sports video game in the world being one about soccer, not about the NBA as one might have guessed, and European people he used to work with who were also really into soccer and an old colleague who was also from England who ended up falling back on the bathtub and hitting his head on the bathtub and dying and he thinks he was actually drunk, but hey, it could happen to anyone, can I honestly tell him that I don't have a drink every once in a while, we all do, though he actually suspects that the English colleague who died was having a lot of problems with his wife and this is what drove him to drink so much and lead to his subsequent fatal accident and, oh man, the food in England really sucks, every time they have potluck here in the hospital the English girl who works in x ray brings something nasty and, tell you what, those Italians have the best food, judging by Maria's in reception potluck contributions and he should set me up with her if I'm ever going to eat any decent food, or, hey, actually do I already have a girlfriend?

And after all this sports and bitches talk I just don't have it in my heart to disappoint him and tell him I'm gay and say, yes, yes, I have a girlfriend indeed. 'Ah good deal man', Jimmy says, drops a pair of headphones around my ears and shoves me into the MRI machine, where I proceed to lay still and hear some loud throbbing noises for the next half an hour or so, only marginally obscured by the best hits of the 80s, 90s, and today, as played by DJ Shotgun on a local radio station that I don't recognise.

46

This weekend I'm going to San Francisco because I've really missed walking around in the summertime in thick London fog wishing I were someplace else, plus I have good friends there that I want to see. On Friday afternoon my flight is scheduled for 2pm, but there has never been an airplane that flew between Los Angeles and San Francisco that wasn't delayed, so I track the status of my flight online, and leave home two hours after the original time. Then, by the time I get to the airport and my gate, I discover that they have moved the flight forward by half an hour again, so, naturally, I've missed it. I sit there for a bit considering whether this is really worth it, whether I really want to go, but the alternative of walking out of that airport, getting a taxi, and going back to Venice, which would take an hour, is too much to handle right now, so I talk to a bored airline person and get moved onto the next flight.

On the way to the next gate I stop at the bathroom and jerk off over the picture of a Hungarian wrestler that someone texted me as part of a Buzzfeed article about big legs being now more important than having a built upper body, which is called "Thighceps Are The New Biceps", and then I sit on the floor against a wall because I think this makes me seem a lot cooler than sitting on a chair and read my book while I wait.

As the people gather around waiting to board, there are two men that stand out. One of them is tall and muscular and he's wearing a tight shirt with very short sleeves, which are showing off his biceps, and tight unfashionable jeans. His face is acceptable, although without the body he would be a definite no. The other guy is also tall, maybe even slightly taller than the first one at a suspected 6'3", and he's also big but his body is a lot softer and he's not wearing clothes to highlight it. His face is more handsome and less Mediterranean and I guess I'm very mature this Friday afternoon, because in the competition I have started in my head about which guy is hotter, the guy with the worse body and better face, wins.

Then we all get on the flight and like it only happens in books with underdeveloped storylines and pornographic films, I am sitting right next to the tall, handsome guy. Then the tall, handsome guy asks me what one of my tattoos means and from that point on, over the course of the next forty-five minutes or however long the flight to San Francisco lasts, everyone around us enjoys a very intimate and embarrassing conversation where we each find out what the other person does, where he lives, where he's going to, where he works out (of course), what siblings he has, and which hand he jerks off with. After we've landed, we walk out towards the exit together, he asks for my number, and I give it to him.

Minutes after we go our separate ways, he sends me the following text:

"Hi, it's Justin. Thanks for the number. It was nice sitting next to you. This whole thing was a very pleasant surprise. I'd like to hang out with you again."

I write back:

"Hey. It was great meeting you. Would love to hang out. Enjoy your stay in SF."

The oddest thing about all this, of course, is that this is an attractive gay guy around my age who lives in Los Angeles and I've never come across before. In fact, it seems almost impossible. But, you know, I have found love on the plane and I'm not going to question it any further. Then I decide to question it a little bit further, so I text Peter and another friend of mine, Kevin, who have lived in LA much longer than I have, and ask them if they know of a guy called Justin, who works for a bank, is in his late 30s, originally from San Diego, and lives in Hollywood. Then twenty minutes later and having confirmed that this is the correct guy via comparing the phone number we all have for him, I have found out that both Peter and Kevin have slept with him, that he is a loon, his body is unsalvageable, and has some very weird fetishes. Then Justin starts texting me asking if I'm free to hang to hang while we're in San Francisco and also that he wants to devour my ass and dominate me in his hotel room either this evening or tomorrow evening, whichever works for me best, and then I haven't found love anymore and I stop responding.

In San Francisco some things happen and none of those things are important, and then it's Sunday afternoon and I'm at the airport again catching my flight back to LA. This is not a flight that Justin is on, and I am very thankful for that, so instead I have the pleasure of sitting next to a middle-aged lady, possibly in her early 50s, whose overly applied mascara and youthful knee-length boots imply that she is a recent divorcee starved for romance. The bouquet of flowers she is parading around like a trophy indicates that she's just found it.

Then, as we wait on the runway to take off, she gets her phone out and types the following message to a contact saved as "Nick [heart emoji] Weller" and I momentarily I think that I'm sitting next to a preteen girl on tumblr, apart from she writes it in all caps and she uses her right index finger to type slowly whilst holding the phone with her left hand far away from her face, which confirms that she is, in fact, in her 50s:

"I DON'T HAVE WORDS TO EXPRESS WHAT I FEEL MAYBE BECAUSE I THINK THAT WHAT WE HAVE IS SO SO SO SO SPECIAL"

Then she follows that up with:

"Sorry"

Nick [heart emoji] Weller doesn't feel that she needs to apologise because he feels the same way and they go back and forth like that for a bit, like drunk puppies and then we are practically racing down the runway and she texts:

"I am yours."

He texts back:

"I am yours."

And then she turns her phone off and we shoot into the sky.

I could read my book during the flight, but I could also watch the love-struck divorcee go through her gallery of pictures with Nick from the weekend they've just spent together and the latter is a lot more entertaining, so I do that. Dozens of pictures of an older gentleman with a thick grey moustache in a denim vest, the two together frolicking around a vineyard, then a deserted beach, all culminating into a series of selfies where they're making out while she steals glances at the camera making sure they're both in shot, so disturbing that I can't pull my eyes away.

Then eventually we land and she beats even me in turning her phone back on, where she immediately checks Facebook to see how the picture of them together she posted is doing (sunset, both smiling weatherworn smiles at the camera – a dignified shot at least and not one of the kissing ones) before she's even read the messages that he's sent while we were flying.

There's a lot of movement in the place now as everyone is trying to get the hell out and I can't see her phone at all times, but I do catch a message where she types, "So kind, So tender, So strong, So everything", complete with funky punctuation and this is enough to lose faith in humanity now and forever. We're also so dumb. We're all so sad. We're also so desperate. And we're all so fucking lonely.

47

There's a restaurant in Venice that I provide as the answer to what my favourite restaurant in Venice is, but in the last couple of times that I went there I was turned away because I was wearing a tank top and they said that they have a no tank tops rule, and I wasn't so sure that this was actually the case or they just didn't want me to be there because I have this delusion of persecution and generally like victimising myself, so on Friday afternoon I go online and check their website and find out that the dress code is real and they're not actually singling me out and refusing me entry. Then I go there and have dinner.

After dinner I walk down to the beach and between the hours of, say, 10.30pm and 12.30am I lay on a beach towel right next to lifeguard tower number 10, feet away from the ocean, in the dark, only illuminated by an iPhone screen going through a playlist that includes *Lemonade* by Sophie, *Novacane* by Frank Ocean, *Burning Up* by Madonna, *Turn Down For What* by Lil Jon and *When Doves Cry* by Prince and, occasionally, by the blinding light the beach patrol is directing at me every time they drive by. There is absolutely nothing better to do on this planet and this is coming from someone with as much of a broken spirit and devoid of joy as myself, so please take my word for it.

For the rest of the weekend I decide that I don't want to see anyone or do anything, which is like the rest of the time really, but at least on this occasion I'm pretending that this is a conscious decision that I made instead of a situation imposed on me by the circumstances, so it's my way of taking the power back. Playing these mind games on yourself is something you can easily perfect when you spend as much time alone as I do. It's like that cat meme on the internet where you supposedly can't outsmart your cat because your cat has all the time in the world to sit there and just wait for you and plot against you, while you're busy with other stuff like going to work, living life, and seeing other people. I am the cat. And also I'm the owner because there's nobody else to plot against. The whole thing is unhealthy.

On Saturday night I'm lying on my sofa watching Netflix and eating ice cream practicing for Saturday nights over the next few decades, and then somebody knocks on my door. It's past 11pm.

I open the door in my underwear. It's Elvira from next-door. She's holding a cup containing two bunches of an unidentified herb that's burning, producing a light, not unpleasant smelling smoke. She tells me that it's sage and that it will help clear out evil spirits if I take it around my apartment. I ask whether I have to do this in every room and she says yes, I should do it now and I can bring the cup back to her when I'm done.

I take the cup with the burning herb and half close the door because I'm not sure whether she wants to stand there and wait while I do this, or whether I have to go to her apartment when I'm done. She then walks away and I understand that I have to go next-door to return it. I walk around with the cup in my living room, kitchen, then the fire has mostly gone out and there's hardly any smoke anymore, but I still take the cup to the bathroom and also walk into my bedroom, so that enough time has passed to prove that I actually did this when I go back. I walk out and go next-door. Her door is ajar. I knock lightly and return the cup to her. She talks to me a bit more about sage and asks me what I'm doing right now and tells me that I can always visit with her more, if I like. I tell her that right now I'm watching a film and I have to go back soon and she asks me what the film is. I tell her I'm watching Annie Hall and she tells me she thought of Diane Keaton earlier today and that her Father once wrote a movie that Diane Keaton was in. I am now standing in her living room, barefoot, still in my underwear. She asks me if I smoke weed and I say no, and she tells me a little bit about some projects that she's currently involved in, something to do with local government, some proof reading stuff, some invites that she has to put together for an event, etc. I ask if she knows who moved into the previously empty apartment opposite mine, and she says she thinks it's an Asian girl, but she's not sure, she doesn't like to gossip about the neighbours, but she did see a small androgynous person come out of the apartment recently and this androgynous person was Asian and visiting the person who's just moved in, and so yes, she thinks it's an Asian girl that moved in. I remind her of my film and she gives me one of the bunches of sage to keep burning in my apartment if I like, then I leave, go back, leave the burnt out sage on the kitchen counter and go lie on my sofa again and press play on Annie Hall, which I had previously paused.

48

A group of us have come to Palm Springs because one of Peter's friends has a house there and he lets him use this house whenever he wants and we thought it might be a good idea to go there for the weekend. Peter and Hunter, who's my new best friend, and three of Peter's friends that I don't know that well drove from LA on Friday, but I decided to stay the night and leave on Saturday, therefore committing to only one night's sleep in the Palm Springs house, because there is a total of six people staying there and I don't know what the sleeping arrangements are, how many rooms there are, how many beds, and that's very stressful to me.

When I get there at Saturday lunchtime all these people are tripping on mushrooms in the back yard around the pool and I don't feel like taking any hallucinogenics ever, so I suppose I'm glad I missed that. They all slowly come around and I get to hear all about their experiences and how the shapes and the colours were moving, and two of Peter's friends who brought the mushrooms have done them before, obviously, and they love this sort of experience, but for Peter and Hunter and the third guy (Nick?) it was their first time and they say they won't be doing it again.

We hang around at the house for most of the day, play music, drink, take some other drugs, order some food, eat it, and then we go out.

It's very unfortunate that when we do go out to what is the only main bar in Palm Springs, Lloyd is also there with his friends from LA, and this is not very unusual because everyone just takes weekends to Palm Springs every now and then, but I would have hoped that someone in my group of friends who have known this and protected me from it, but I guess they didn't know and they didn't. When I see Lloyd my heart clenches and I don't want to be there anymore and luckily Hunter and Peter understand this, so Hunter and I leave this bar (Peter stays there with his three friends) and go to the Ace Hotel, where someone's heard there's a party.

The Ace party is kinda dead and there are too many straight people but at least there are some gay people we know from LA there too and these are better ones than Lloyd and his friends. In fact, the people we know from LA are Daniel, Rus, and X, the throuple that initially flew in Lloyd to LA all that time ago and had a sex weekend with him. I guess they're no longer on friendly terms or even if they are on friendly terms, they're not hanging out together this weekend. So Hunter and I join their group and we all exchange drugs and then one things leads to another and one hour later Daniel, Rus, X, Hunter, a random new guy that Rus found on Grindr and I are hanging out naked in the hot tub back at the house where we're staying and everyone is high off their faces and starts fucking, and this is fine, because previously I thought that Daniel and Rus and X didn't like me for some reason, so, politically and socially, this small orgy is definitely a good idea and we will all come out on the other side liking each other a lot better. The addition of the sixth person is also genius, because he operates as a great buffer, for example, when you turn around and there's somebody there that you already know and have some history with and you don't feel like putting your dick inside right now, you grab the stranger, put him in the middle and the awkwardness is averted. Then everyone cums and passes out and I don't know where everyone sleeps or what happens when Peter comes back to the house with his three friends after their night out, because after all the sex is over around 4am, I decide that I'm done and I drive back to LA by myself.

JULY 2014

49

On Tuesday it's a very busy day because I have to get my haircut and also go and sit on the beach for a few hours to work on my tan before going away this weekend, so I wake up very early and make my way to the barbershop around 11am. I think every man in America had his haircut last week in preparation for the 4th of July weekend, so the shop is empty from clients this morning and two of the barbers are giving haircuts to each other, while the other two are just sitting around watching baseball on the big TV screen. I seriously cannot comprehend the amount of baseball these people are willing to consume.

The head barber, who is by far the loudest and most stupid out of all of them and is currently having his haircut by one of the apprentices, is revealed to have a tattoo covering the sides and back of his head. It's only becoming visible now, because he's getting his hair shaved off. I can't tell what it's meant to portray, it's just a smudge of indistinguishable shapes, but it's there and it's very big. I'd be lying if I said that I don't find this somewhat of a turn-on, because it confirms he's complete trash, and I'd probably be developing a crush on him right now, were it not for the fact that otherwise he looks like a burrito.

Halfway through my haircut by the quiet, mild-mannered Mateo, another client walks in and sits down to have his cut by the fourth barber. During the small talk, the client mentions that he's about to start plumbing school. He's a typical LA Latino teen with tattoos, key chains, and pulled up black sports socks. He says that he's looking forward to it, but complains that it's so expensive and had to take out a loan to pay for the fees. The head barber overhears all this, tells him that he'll take the money instead and this is all he needs to know about plumbing:

"Shit flows downwards. Don't bite your nails while you work. Payday's on Friday."

Sweet Mateo finishes my haircut and I ride my bike down to the beach.

There are a few people around, it's not overly crowded, but I choose a spot not far from an obnoxious gym guy with huge traps, a giant ass, an American flag towel and a black Labrador, who's running around like crazy and creating a huge scene. Of course you are not allowed to bring dogs to the beach, so I'm now obsessed with the guy. I sit down and start taking discreet pictures of him and snapchatting them to all my friends adding really sexually aggressive comments. At one point, the dog sits on the guy's towel and when he sees this from 100 feet away, he throws his hand up exasperated and shouts:

"Bro!"

The dog pays no notice, but I do.

I sit there going through a playlist comprising the debut albums of Sky Ferreira, Black Flag, Notorious B.I.G., and Joy Division on shuffle, and when that's done and I'm satisfied with the amount of sun I've got, I go home.

In the evening, I'm still so upset by the existence of the beach guy with the dog that I decide to skip the gym.

I listen to some records and read a bit of my book and waste time on dating apps and when I receive the following message in response to the "Hey man, how yoy doing this evenin" I send to a random guy on Scruff, I decide that it's time to go to bed:

"I'm a very well traveled, athletic, passionate, smart guy. Love personal one on one competition. All kinds of sports. I am not a communist, a socialist, a liberal or a gay-centric person, I am a real American man that strives to be the best at what ever I am doing without blaming others for my downfalls and travails. I am not 420 friendly. I am not a victim. I love and respect my straight male friends and expect any gay men I hang with to do the same. I am probably a lot stronger than you. Armwrestling a hot, built guy is more thrilling to me than fucking or sucking. Trading gut punches with a guy gets me hard. When I drive I grip the top of my steering wheel high and tight so my tricep muscle is shown off to any dude who happens to pull along side of me, I am amazed at how many guys will respond in kind and show off as well. I travel too much to have a lover but would love to find one someday that can compete with me, travel with me and be smart enough (or dumb enough) to keep me interested. Having sex with me first time out of the gate will be the first and last time, be physical with me through sports and activities and ease into it guys if you ever want a chance for a longer relationship. I am ok with getting at each other instantly if the chem is right but don't get pissed when I don't follow up, just the way I am wired, I am a hunter not a collector. Most of my friends are straight males and females. I don't go to gay bars or have rainbow flags at my door or on my smart car or prius. I have a pickup, several bikes, a 1968 Shelby Cobra. I own several guns and know how to use them. I have several fishing poles and know how to use them. I own power tools and know how to use them. I also know what $Z = \cos\theta_W\ W_3 - \sin\theta_W\ B$ means. I can hang with construction workers, billionaire hedge fund guys, archeologists, astrophysicists, Mary Kay entrepreneurs, doctors, sports celebs, politicians of all parties, women, men and children and can entertain them all. I can camp in a tent above 12,000 feet and completely enjoy it. I also enjoy my time at the Amangiri desert pool suite. I learn how to live and make my life better from the successful and wealthy. I learn how not live my life from the poor. Both are my friends. I have never gotten a job or a project from someone poorer than me. I have, however, been introduced to someone who has given me a job or a project from someone poorer than me. I am most comfortable with wickedly and insanely intelligent people (the kind that are so smart they don't have a clue about themselves or the rest of us), or the complete opposite dummy with out much education. One stimulates my brain the other relaxes it. I am aggressive and get off on guys that are also mutually aggressive. Effeminate and gay centric guys turn me off. Submissive guys turn me off. Fat, overweight guys turn me off. Muscle turns me on. Lean muscle turns me on even more. How the hell are you doing this evening?"

50

On Friday morning way before it's acceptable to open up your eyes and leave your bed I wake up and call an Uber to make my way to the airport. My flight leaves at 11.30am. I'm going to Canada for my good friend Ryan's wedding. Ryan used to live in London and we dated, of course, for a few weeks and then we didn't date anymore. This was years ago. Then we became friends and then everyone moved to different places around the world and fell in and out of love with several different people, but during that process Ryan met somebody that was willing to stop and marry him, so now I'm going to their wedding.

When my Uber to the airport arrives, I'm lucky enough that my driver is a Ukrainan immigrant (yes, I know I've mistyped Ukrainan, but give me one good reason to type it correctly) who's been in the US for seven months and is an aspiring stand-up comedian. In very broken English. I don't ask details about his move to the US or how he's allowed to live here, because I feel that from a legal point of view, I'm in a much less precarious position not knowing a thing. Then the Ukrainan Uber driver and stand-up comedian tries some of his jokes on me and I can't say I remember all of them, but I certainly remember a couple of them and those are:

"I was in the church the other day ushering. An old woman came in and said, 'Where should I sit?' I told her to sit at the back in the last two rows. She said, 'Do you know who I am?' and I said, 'No, thank god!'" (End of joke)

"I had a weird passenger the other day. I went to a house and the woman there gave me a soup and said, 'Will you deliver this to my friend who's sick?' I said 'Yeah, a soup as a passenger, what great company. The soup is cool and it's cool. Get it? It's cool company and it's cool in temperature" (End of joke)

Then we get to the airport.

By the time I get to the east coast of Canada most of the day has passed, plus it's three hours later here, apparently, because that's how the planet works, and then suddenly I'm at Canadian border control. The immigration person gives me a hard time, which is surprising as she's a girl my age or younger and I expect her to just flirt with me and wave me through, but I suppose that's just because I'm conceited and sexist, and sometimes these attributes might bite you in the ass. She doesn't like the fact that I'm traveling on my own, she doesn't like the fact that I'm meeting friends here (how can I possibly know these people if they live there and I live in LA, she asks, like she's never been to a circuit party before) she doesn't like the fact that my job is only part-time. Then she slowly comes to terms with all those things and she lets me in.

Then I find myself on a shuttle bus being driven to the resort where the wedding is taking place, 75 miles east of Ottawa. This is an adventure sports resort with water rafting, kayaking, and bungee-jumping facilities because Ryan and his new husband-to-be are very masculine, so my driver is a 20-year-old rafting instructor in a beat up van. Unfortunately he is not as hot as that sounds. He does spend the next couple of hours talking to me about his outdoorsy lifestyle though, how he chases the summer around the world, works at different resorts, teaches people how to raft, does all sorts of other hospitality jobs for free shelter and food and quite possibly a constant supply of weed, and I must be getting really old because none of this sounds appealing to me.

When we get to the resort he takes me to the cabin where I'm staying with a number of other people that I know from circuiting around the world, some South Africans I met in London, some New Yorkers I met in Miami, some Canadians I met on Instagram, and we all get high on some terrible coke someone flew in with from Toronto and drunk on whatever leftover drinks are laying around from the welcoming party I missed because I got here at 11pm.

On Saturday morning I wake up at 9am with the rest of my house and we go get breakfast, and you have to admire their courage, because they still manage to make their water rafting adventure between 10am-2pm, while I go back to bed taking prescription sleeping pills that I acquired from three different people and passing out until the late afternoon.

In the evening we all get dressed up and stand around in groups and bitch about each other, but never about the grooms, who have an incredible amount of goodwill in their favour at the moment, and very rightly so. Then we watch them get married. People make some great speeches, about love, about companionship, about the progress of gay rights in the last few years, and I'd like to feel bitter and mock all those things because I'm just so cynical, but I can't, it's all pretty great and I want a wedding like that for myself pretty much immediately, thanks.

Then my group finds some GHB and some MDMA and also lots more drinks, and then we dance and talk and hug and then I make out with three people and one of them sucks me off in a field behind the tent where the wedding reception is taking place and he seems to be very persistent that I cum in his mouth so he makes a really good effort for what seems like a very long time but I can't finish because I'm way too high, and then we return to the tent and I take some more G and then I start collapsing and my friends from South Africa take me back to the cabin where we're staying and give me some coke to wake me up and then I wake up and I'm quite sober and the guy from the field is now also here at the cabin with a large number of the wedding guests who have moved the party from the tent to our home and the guy wants to continue with all the oral sex but I'm really tired and over it, so I suck him off and take his load in my mouth quickly to get him off my back and then I swallow some sedatives and fall asleep on a bench right outside the cabin facing a lake, while everyone else continues to party around me.

51

On the Monday after the wedding weekend instead of going back to LA, I catch a flight and travel to London instead, because I was already half way there, so why not. I guess I'm coming down from all sorts of recreational activities over the weekend and this is not a fun flight at all and I'm really depressed right now about a multitude of things, but one of them is, of course, my single-minded obsession with pretending to want to be in a relationship, and a monogamous relationship at that, and how on earth am I ever going to be able to do that, because I can't name a single long-term relationship that I know in London or LA that doesn't involve some degree of openness.

Then I start getting some messages from this guy I slept with once when he was visiting LA who currently lives in Chicago and he's quite smart, even though he's 28 and still in the closet, and we have kept in touch and right now after I complain a bit about the state of relationships in the big gay scenes that I've always lived in, the conversation goes a bit like this.

Chicago Guy: "Perhaps it's you who can't accept the nature of homosexuality since you want what nobody seems to be willing or able to give. Not your fault for wanting it. It's probably the more noble good."

Me: "That's a good point. Perhaps the nature of homosexuality is eternal adolescence and polygamy."

Chicago Guy: "Yeah actually it really may be. It's not written anywhere that it has to follow the same pattern as heterosexuality."

Chicago Guy: "Since the latter is conducive to raising children and the former is not."

And I don't know who is more homophobic right now: me wanting a relationship that adheres to the heterosexual ideals that I was brought up with or the closeted Chicago guy who presents a theory where homosexuality is never going to be a monogamous state, but I think it really is pretty close.

Then I get to London, where I stay for a week.

On Friday afternoon in London I invite a couple of people over for dinner to the airbnb flat where I'm staying in Covent Garden, two of my closest friends, and when George arrives, naturally, he brings with him a gram of ketamine. We start taking this and become immobilised for a bit and watch *Come Dine With Me* repeats, then Max also arrives and joins us and when we run out he says that he has a surprise and pulls out some pills that his drug dealer gave him for free last time he bought coke and he hasn't tried them before, but we should all take them now. These pills are called Happy-5 or Erinim and I've never heard of them before, but a quick online research shows that they are favoured by Japanese businessmen who originally used to take them to relax because they are generally stressed as fuck, but they are now very popular for recreational use amongst experienced benzo users in Malaysia, Singapore, and Indonesia, and all this sounds like a pretty good recommendation to me. Then we take the pills, leave the flat, and walk around central London for a couple of hours generally feeling pretty chill. Then I go back home and have the best night's sleep in recent memory.

On Saturday night, I go to my friend William's, who's having a pre-party before going out clubbing. There are maybe 8-10 people there. We take all the drugs and head out. We stay in the club for five or six hours, during which I make out with more people than I can count right now and have a quasi-memorable non-penetrative threesome in the dark room with a 24-year-old English guy from up north, who just came out and moved to London less than six months ago and is currently doing the his first gay pride / circuit party summer parade, and an American guy my age who lives in London and is spending the entire night standing in the bathroom with his pants pulled down to his knees, lathering up his dick with water and soap from the sinks with a look in his face indicating he is so high that there is no way he will have any recollection of this the next day and taking breaks to walk into the dark room and have group sex with people he has picked up that way, while his boyfriend (also in the club) is searching for him.

Gay London is going through a wild drugs and sex phase right now, culturally, so much so that a new compound word has been invented to launch a million thinkpieces about gay culture: chemsex. Of course gay London was going through a wild drugs and sex phase even when I was living there ten years ago, but a lot more people are talking about it now, so it must be getting worse? I don't know. Maybe it is, or maybe the mainstream media finally caught up and started writing about it and now it's a self-perpetuating circle. In any case, the dating options that one has between the cities of London and LA are two. Either you choose LA and try to find someone to date in a pool of countless attractive uncultured morons with no job, or you choose London and try to find someone to date who may have a good education and a great job, but prefers to spend every weekend hopping around clubs, "chill-outs" (orgies), after clubs, after-after clubs for sixty hours starting Friday evening, until he gets spat out sleepless, debilitated, and filled with regret at his desk in Canary Wharf on Monday morning just in time to miss his first meeting. There might be normal people in both cities that don't fall within either category, but those people are not in the gay scene, and quite frankly I don't know how to exist outside the gay scene (but will happily blame everyone else for it).

On Sunday evening, I fly back to LA. I'm proud that during this weekend in London I have not concerned myself with Brett at all, nor have I tried to stalk him and see what he's doing with his new boyfriend, even though I'm in the same city as them for the first time since the break up. This must be progress.

AUGUST 2014

52

On Saturday afternoon, I meet up with Jeremy to go to a pool party. Jeremy is somebody I met on Grindr four or five months ago. We hooked up, kept in touch and have had sex a couple more times since. A couple of months after we first met, he started seeing somebody. He never told me this directly, but I found out from other people, because there are only about 200 people in the gym-going gay scene of any big city and we all know each other's business. So despite not telling me, I knew that Jeremy had a boyfriend the last two times we hooked up, but I went ahead and did it anyway, because the guy that Jeremy is currently going out with made out at a party five years ago with somebody I was dating at the time, plus he was sending Lloyd naked pictures on Facebook when Lloyd was still going out with me and living at my place. So I don't feel like I have any reason to be respectful of him and his relationship, and I'm definitely not mature or clever enough to realise that the only reason that I'm as unhappy and emotionally damaged as I am is because I constantly choose to repeat and perpetuate bad behaviours that I previously fell victim too.

Jeremy and I get to the pool party where 150 of our closest friends are, and act vaguely like we're dating, even though everyone knows that Jeremy has a boyfriend and, more importantly, is friends with his boyfriend. I'm guessing that the boyfriend recently did something to piss off Jeremy and I am Jeremy's way to take revenge, and that's fine by me. A few people come say hi to us and ask Jeremy where the boyfriend is, conversations, which I pretend not to hear, because I am still pretending to Jeremy that I don't know he has a boyfriend, even though he knows that I know.

Then we leave and while I'm driving Jeremy home, he gets a phone call from his boyfriend. I only hear Jeremy's side of the conversation:

"Driving around."

"We're going to get some food."

"I'm with a friend."

"Konrad."

"Konrad Platt."

And then the boyfriend hangs up. I imagine this is exactly what Jeremy wanted and he must be very pleased with himself right now. I get to his house, go inside with him, we take a shower together, fuck, and I leave. Outside, I find a parking ticket on my car. I text Jeremy with, "Goddammit, I got a ticket", Jeremy offers to pay for it because it's his street and he should have known where I'm not allowed to park, I say that no, he doesn't have to do that, and I go home.

53

On this empty Wednesday morning I have nothing to do and no one to account to. I could be doing absolutely anything with my freedom of time, anywhere on this planet, so I sit here at my desk and scan my recommended friends tab on Facebook looking for someone to flirt with. I scroll through thumbnail profile pictures of young gay men scattered around the country and click to send a friend request to anyone who stands out. People can stand out by being white, under 45, and having worked out at least three times in the last week. Consequently, eight out of ten people on average in my recommended friends stands out. Online desperation is a game of numbers, apparently, and soon enough a few of these prospects start accepting me and just like that we are now in each other's lives. I click into the profile of a thick-necked Neanderthal called Aaron Wellinger who resides in Little Rock, whatever that is, and see that his last post is from yesterday evening when he uploaded a picture of himself standing in a gym with his shirt off flexing his muscles with the tagline, "Why not". He looks hot as fuck. I google Little Rock to find out where it is and message him:

"Hey man , hows life in Arkansas"

He writes back:

"Hey [smiley emoji]. Not too bad. Cloudy today. How are you"

"I'm good. We're having pretty good weather here in LA. I like your pictures"

"I like yours too"

Then I don't write for a bit because someone buzzes me from downstairs and have to go pick up a delivery and when I come back upstairs I check my messages and Aaron has written:

"You message me and immediately disappear? Typical [winking emoji with tongue sticking out]"

I write back:

"Why do we have to fight all the time? Smh"

Then Aaron decides to continue the conversation by sending four almost identical shirtless pictures of him looking into a mirror, with the only variation being what he's wearing from the waist down. Also, on his head. In one picture he's wearing a pair of black sweat shorts. In the second picture he's wearing just a white towel. In the third picture he's not wearing anything but his dick is obscured by a strategically positioned bathroom sink. In the fourth picture he's wearing a white towel again, but this time he's also wearing a green baseball cap with a bill that's way too curved, but it will have to do.

In response to those, I send him a picture in my underwear, standing in my bedroom looking very angrily into the camera. He then replies with two emojis: a smiley face with two hearts instead of eyes, and a wedding ring. Then he also sends me his number.

We spend the next hour or so talking sexual positions and exchanging dick and ass pictures. Then suddenly, Aaron takes it to the next level and sends me a video, quite unprompted. The video starts with a shot of a bed in an empty room. I understand this is his bedroom. There is a framed illustration of a Little Rock skyline on the wall above his bed, and I only know this because it also includes the words 'Little Rock' written on it. I can also see a vintage Arkansas RiverBlades poster and a couple of whiskey-related framed prints. Then Aaron steps into the frame naked, ass first, facing away from the camera. He walks up to the bed and takes a position on it on all fours. He spends the next twenty seconds or so on his knees curving his lower back up and down and quietly moaning as though he's being fucked by someone invisible. When this is over, he gets up, still facing away so you never get to see his face, walks back closer to the camera, gives a little wave, then a victory sign, and turns it off.

I give him the enthusiastic response he is looking for and a picture of my erect dick. He messages and says that "he wants this to belong to him". I tell him that "the same applies to his ass; mine". He says, "I'm yours baby."

Then I don't message anymore because I think that the conversation has come to a natural end for now, but an hour later he writes, "ouch".

I ask him what's wrong and he complains that I disappeared right after he told me that he wants to be property of Konrad Platt. I apologise and say that I want to meet up. He asks me when it's good, and he'll fly to me whenever I want. He adds that he needs to come visit soon, because he doesn't like the idea of me being with other dudes now that we've met.

We stop talking again and an hour later he sends a second video. The video opens with a close up shot of a dildo, which I believe is positioned on some low piece of furniture in his bedroom. He walks into the frame again in the same manner as the first video, looking away, and proceeds to crouch down, spread his ass open and sit on the dildo. He fucks himself for a bit that way before standing up and giving his signature wave and victory sign, and then the video ends. I ask him why he's doing this to me and add that I want him so bad. He says, "We have to meet ASAP".

Then I go to the gym. An hour later he starts texting me again. He says that he wants me to be serious when I talk about us. That he likes it when I say that I want his butt to be only mine. And that he wants me. I say that I want him too. Then the conversation goes a bit like this.

Aaron: "I have free flights with miles that are earmarked to come see you."

Me: "Let's do it."

Then half an hour later:

Aaron: "So."

Me: "So?"

Aaron: "Nevermind. Good night."

Me: "Wow"

Aaron: "Well"

Me: "Well what?"

Aaron: "Nothing"

Me: "Wow again"

Aaron: "True"

Me: "I'm not sure what's going on in this conversation, but I don't believe it's following any of the social norms I've ever come across before."

Aaron: "Well I'm drunk. You're not being sweet or attentive. So there we are."

Me: "I'm sorry"

The next morning he sends me a text at 7am with a sad face emoji. I happen to be awake and reply, "Where were you last night?"

Aaron says: "At a bar"

Me: "What was happening there?"

Aaron: "Nothing. Was just thirsty."

Me: "What do you think of our conversation last night?"

Aaron: "Can we just not discuss it and pretend it didn't happen please"

Me: "Sure"

Aaron: "Thanks bae"

Aaron: "You mad"

Me: "Yes. I'm very mad. You are not allowed to drink anymore."

Aaron: "Ha. Good luck. So I want more attention from you. Big deal"

Me: "I mean"

Aaron: "Be nice. Isn't a hangover punishment enough?"

Then I fall back asleep and wake up at 10am. He texts me around 11am with a frowning emoji. I text back with an emoji with a straight line for a mouth.

Aaron: "You my bae"

Me: "You are mine forever. You are my love"

Aaron: "That's the kind of stuff I want you to be serious about"

Me: "But Aaron. Let me level with you. We have exchanged, like, ten messages. We have only spoken for a day. I do think you're incredibly sexy. And you also seem nice, etc. But we don't know each other yet. And I don't understand how we can go from 'meeting' online one day to saying these things to each other the next. It's odd. Even if the promise is there, I don't believe these things when you say them and I don't want to say them back because they are hollow and not true. I just don't understand what you want us to do right now. And that's everything."

Aaron: "It's cool. Just don't message me anymore though. Take care dude."

Then I block his number, block him on Facebook, and go to bed.

54

On Wednesday evening I'm leaving my flat to go to the gym and I'm at the stage where I'm holding my bike, I've put my headphones in, started my music and pressed the button for the lift. This is a daring move on my part, because I don't want to be rude and usually wait to start the music until after I've exited the main entrance of the building downstairs, just in case I come across a neighbour inside the building and they happen to say hello or make any other conversation and I miss it because I'm listening to some song. Of course the one time when I have taken my chances and started playing my music immediately upon exiting my flat, Elvira, my next-door neighbour opens her door, shouts my name and comes out. I don't know if there's a facial expression when your heart sinks, but if there is, I'm wearing it right now. I stop the music and courteously pull one headphone out.

Elvira is holding a joint but she quickly puts it out using her finger, which is highly alarming, an unquestionable sign of psychopathy and indicates that this woman is not fazed by fire, so I can't imagine that my mildly annoyed glare will have any greater effect. As is our usual dynamic, I am prepared to not say anything, and just listen. I did contribute to the conversation one time and that one time I told her that I was born in Germany and this seemed highly exotic to her and she started asking me several questions about Germany, and when I pointed out I haven't lived in Germany in twenty years and to be honest I don't even know what goes on there anymore she wasn't deterred and now she brings up Germany at least 90% of the time that she sees me.

"I wanted to ask to ask you, what do the Germans think of the Greek election?" she asks, grinning like a loon.

I look over at the lift door automatically closing behind me, shutting away my only escape route, breathe out a heavy sigh and say, "What election?"

The neighbour goes on to explain that there was a recent election for President or Prime Minister in Greece, "whatever they have over there", and the party that got elected will stick it to Europe and particularly Germany (they'll say "fuck you" to Germany, she says) and will fight for their independence and they're badass motherfuckers and won't put up with all the debt shit anymore. Haven't I heard?

I shake my head to indicate that I haven't.

She continues for a bit and tells me how proud she is of the Greeks for voting for independence and then she performs a little Greek dance to demonstrate her solidarity, an act that involves her raising her arms to the sides and clicking her fingers whilst doing a few steps of something that approximates what she might have seen in a movie, right there in our building corridor.

At that point, as an instinctive reaction, I drop my bike sideways on the floor. This may have been involuntary, but it serves as a survival technique, because it interrupts her delirium and gives me an out. She swiftly moves on from performing the dance of Zorba The Greek to leaning over my bike and mock-stroking its handles, whispering "poor bike, you're not hurt, are you?" as I maniacally press the button for the lift again, which comes just in time when I've picked up the bike and I'm ready to go.

As the lift door closes once again with me inside this time, I hear her shout in perfect clarity: "Of course you don't know anything about the Greek election, you American, you", her tone dripping in mockery.

I ride four miles to the gym, work out chest and biceps, first next to a very hot homophobic bro who moves away after one set when I approach him to work in with him, then next to a very hot bi/curious bro who approaches me to work in with me as soon as the first bro leaves, and ride four miles back home, listening to my iPod on shuffle which brings up the following sequence of songs: *Liar* by Henry Rollins, *Say My Name* by Destiny's Child, *Mistaken For Strangers* by The National, a live version of *Declare Independence* by Björk, *Denis* by Blondie, and *Seeing Other People* by Belle And Sebastian.

55

On Wednesday morning I wake up in the afternoon, do some non-urgent work and then walk down to the beach a few hours later. It's not really that hot today. Nobody interesting is around. I sit there and attempt to catch some sun despite all the clouds, listening to Sufjan Stevens, latter-day Blur, and b-sides from Vespertine, because I'm in that kind of self-pitying mood. I open Instagram and scroll through my timeline. One of several hundred empty shells that I follow, whose only job in life is to work out and patronise me with motivational quotes on social media, has posted a black and white picture of himself standing in a gym locker room eye-fucking the camera, with his left hand on his hip and the right arm raised up to lean gently against a door frame, in a transparent attempt to showcase his armpit, which is actually working in creating all sorts of sensations in my lower abdomen. To drive the point home, he is flexing every inch of his body. I stare at the picture for a few seconds and then click into his profile to remind myself who he is. His bio reads "OCB men's physique competitor, male model, fitness advocate". I switch to my web browser quickly and look up "OCB", which I now know stands for "Organization of Competitive Bodybuilders". I go back into the Instagram app and look at more pictures, trying to figure out whether he's gay. The results are inconclusive. There are mixed posts of him with his arm around "hot" girls (although never the same one twice) and posts of him working as a shirtless barman in what looks like a gay bar. What am I supposed to think? I go back to today's post, the black and white picture, and read the blurb he's written for it:

"5 years ago, I entered a drought of happiness. I suffered from general anxiety, panic attacks, and depression. I overthought everything, and was hyper-sensitized all the time. Irrational thoughts lingered in my head. I was lost. With the help of family, friends, and my own desire to recover I went through a self-help program and did my own meditation, readings, and reflections. As miserable as the experience was I would go through it all again, for what I learned is forever valuable. Happiness is all relative. A human brain is nearly identical in all humans, meaning it will produce the same amount of neurotransmitter as every other brain. No matter what you possess, what happens to you, your happiness is all up to you. How you choose to perceive what your situation is, is exactly that, a CHOICE. If you engage in positive self talk, and love yourself unconditionally, then regardless of what's happening you will find mental stability. Once you comprehend this idea it's interesting what you will find yourself achieving."

He has followed that up with the hashtags, #innerpeace #strongmind #strongbody #itsallmental #pump #fitfam #traininsane #perspective #iseverything

Despite finding it a little insensitive that he should include the hashtag #traininsane in his public service announcement about mental health, I am relieved to know that the cure to all psychological issues is to go to the gym and become swoll as fuck, so I leave the beach and go to the gym.

On Wednesday evening after the gym I'm sitting at my desk doing some more work, which primarily consists of trying to learn all the lyrics to a twee punk album called *Quarterbacks* by a band called Quarterbacks, when I hear a knock on my door.

I open it expecting to see my next-door neighbour, Elvira, but this time it's not my next-door neighbour, it's her next-door neighbour from the other side. This neighbour is another middle-aged lady who has been abusing the rent control system for the last quarter of a century. Her name is Linda.

Linda hands me a mobile phone and tells me that Elvira wants to talk to me. On the phone, Elvira tells me that she's away for a few weeks and that while she's been away, somebody's tried to break into her apartment by taking a window screen down and opening the blinds. That's as far as they went. Now, there are always many questions when Elvira is involved and there aren't ever any answers, so I don't even bother asking them this time. The questions that form in my head and quickly disappear on this occasion are: a) why would anyone want to break in and steal a bunch of half-burnt sage, a pile of old newspapers from 1978, and 25-years' worth of dust (I've been inside the apartment, I know what's in there), b) why would anyone pull the screen and open the blinds then give up their pathetic attempt at a burglary, it's not like I or any other neighbour would care enough to stop them, and finally, c) what do I have to do with this.

Before this conversation goes any further Linda tells me that she wants her phone back and can I give Elvira my number so she can call me directly? And just like that, Linda is out, that crafty bitch, and Elvira has my number and my life is over.

Then Elvira calls me directly and tells me about her burglary nightmare and I'm convinced that despite being away she's actually orchestrated this just to create some building drama because she's bored and high somewhere faraway and she feels like she's losing her tight grip on her territory, the only place that she feels like she fully controls, our apartment building. In any case, my role in this, I find out, is to go over, wearing some gloves in order to protect any fingerprints, and pull the screen back up and close the blinds. I don't know in which order.

I say yes that I'll go over and do that. I come out of my apartment and walk to the crime scene and Linda is standing there, hunchbacked, joyless, and mousy, and tells me that perhaps I shouldn't touch anything, gloves or no gloves, but I should tell Elvira to call the police first. Then I go back to my apartment and call Elvira to make this suggestion to her. Elvira freaks out and says that this sounds like a Linda idea, is it a Linda idea? Linda is such a meddler. I admit that, yes, this was a Linda idea. Elvira then goes on to say that she doesn't want police anywhere near her apartment, not for any reason, she doesn't want anyone in her apartment as a matter of fact, well OK, the police in particular, because of certain things she's got in there. She lets out a brief conspiratory chuckle when she says this, and I'm not sure what I'm conspiring to, because this can range from anything like bagfuls of weed (a certainty) to decomposing, badly maintained bodies (a very strong possibility).

So anyway, the police are out, we can never call them, but I do have to go over again and close the blinds and also put tape all over the window. I don't have any tape, I say. She says, fine, do it later, can you put a note up on the door for the time being though, and I say, sure I can do that, what do you want the note to say. She says to me, are you writing this down, I can spell out any words if you don't know how to spell them because you're foreign, and I know what you foreigners are like. This is from a woman that really needs my help right now. I say, no I think I'll be fine, and she dictates: "this unit is under surveillance". At the end of that she starts spelling out "surveillance" to me anyway: "s…u…r…v…e…y…" Then she tells me some more about burglars in general, because we've now all signed up to this ridiculous conceit apparently that "burglars" did this, and the she gets off the phone.

I write her loony phrase on the back of a white envelope, which is the only piece of blank paper I have at home, and come out of my apartment again, where I see Linda standing there with some tape in one hand and her phone on the other. Linda tells me that here's the tape I'll need to stick the note on the door, she knows I don't have any (Elvira called her immediately after we stopped talking and let her know of my failings) and I can also use it to tape over the window if I want.

I take the tape, stick the envelope on the door, leave the tape on Linda's doorstep and go back to my apartment. I have three missed calls from Elvira and a voicemail. I delete the voicemail without listening to it and go fill my bathtub.

56

On Friday I'm casually texting Peter regarding my plans for the day.

Me: "I just ate more than I could handle, because gains. Heading to the gym. Pray for me that at least two of my straight crushes are there, please."

Peter: "Praying. Though wait a second. You didn't go yesterday, did you? Do you really want to see them after having missed a day?"

Me: "Now I'm panicking."

Peter: "I'm kidding. I hope that they're there and they ask you for tips."

Me: "I hope that they're there and they give me the straight acceptance my Father never did."

Peter: "I hope that for you as well."

Me: "Ty."

I go to the gym and do a half-arsed workout of shoulders and calves, and yes this is a unique training combination I have just invented, and then I drive to the store, and then I drive home. I drove to the gym instead of riding my bike there, because today it's raining. At least this provides some novelty in our otherwise dire existences. It also provides the opportunity for the usual five or six people to post on Facebook about how much they like the rain, the storm, the rain clouds, the wet streets, the grey skies, etc. They like it all. Because they're deep, you see? They operate on a higher level than the rest of us, who just like it to be sunny every day. Of course these people who write these posts…every… time…it rains…have never lived anywhere else other than Southern California and wouldn't move anywhere else either. I personally want to invite them to move to London for one season, say, one spring, and see what their views on the rain as a meteorological phenomenon and its effects one one's disposition will be then. Just one season.

Back at home I cook something to eat while listening to a Björk remix from 1993 that is making me really, really happy, when I receive a text from Kevin. Kevin is also home alone, because we all are. We all are alone. Unless you are an idiot or really poor after you're 30 and need to have roommates, in which case you have even more problems to deal with, but you don't know it yet. You're too busy chilling or getting drunk with your roommates still, and you'll find out what a loser you are in your mid-30s, possibly early 40s when life has passed you by and you end up alone. But not Kevin or I. Kevin and I know what losers we are now, and we are already alone.

Kevin recently went on a few dates with a young idiot on steroids, who's actually quite attractive and could be used as a trophy boyfriend, if that's what you're after, but you know he has nothing to give back to you. Plus he's in his late 20s and only moved to LA in the past year, so there's no hope of him having a relationship with somebody. Despite all this and despite them having nothing in common, because this younger guy, Brandon, has the exact personality and depth of the back cover on the last book Kevin read (paperback) I suppose Kevin is also chasing them trophy boyfriends, or perhaps he's exclusively thinking with his dick and nothing else, and who can blame him, Kevin thought that they could be boyfriends. So Kevin took Brandon out on several dates, cooked for him, tried to connect, and they did for a while, then the guy got bored and he started flaking. And he doesn't initiate plans, he cancels dates, he's slowly disappearing.

Now Kevin is complaining.

"I'm going to do all the G you've left at my house tonight and kill myself."

I text back:

"Oh? Why, what's happening?"

"I tried to use it to lure Brandon over tonight. But Weho twunks were more appealing I guess."

"What's the latest with that?"

"He's being all sweet, but he isn't really trying to close the deal. I'm being aloof but responsive."

"All right. So let me ask. Outside the physical attraction, do you have a connection with this person? Do you have common interests, things to talk about?"

"Ish. We have shared experiences. What's ur point?"

"Why all this effort?"

"There isn't much effort."

Then Kevin continues:

"I wasn't even that attracted to Brandon."

Yeah right.

"And, I'm not very upset about it. I've slept like a rock all week. I'm more lamenting the general lack of people to date."

"There is a definite lack of people to date."

Then Kevin takes a picture of the dinner he's cooked, a dinner that would feed two people, if Brandon had turned up, sends it to me and says:

"I am eating for 2."

"We need to find you a boyfriend."

"Hope he likes fat guys."

Now, earlier in the day I took a picture of myself lying flat on my dinner table with my face against it and posted it on Instagram with the comment "high drama". So I say to Kevin:

"Why don't you outpour on Instagram with a dramatic headshot against a wooden surface?"

"Been done."

"You need to find your own USP, I guess. Who are you? Why should someone date you? Find it. Post it. They will come flocking in."

"What is a USP?"

"Unique selling point."

"I'm kind, handsome, and smart. That's what I've been selling for years. I guess I need to work on the unique part."

"Yeah you need something else, sorry."

Then I explain to Kevin that he needs to decide who the person that he is is, and drive it home, via social media. What's my USP? I ask him. I'm tragic and beautiful. I'm like those dumb, worked out people, but I'm just so smart and tortured, you know? Instant USP. What's Lloyd M.'s USP? He's a genuine, down to earth guy with strict morals, who loves sports, country and family, but happens to be gay. That's his USP right there. Now, of course our intended USP might be interpreted differently than we want it by the wider audience, but it still counts. So instead of highly intelligent self-aware gym guy, the majority of people might look at me and think "self-absorbed queen who thinks he's smarter than he is". For Lloyd, the majority might sum it up briefly as "self-loathing dumb jock". That's fine. These are just semantics. The recipients of the message will still get it, and will still want to fuck you.

Kevin gets it, but he's being lazy so he asks:

"Why don't you think of my USP?"

I take a few seconds, restart my beloved Björk remix for what must be the fifteenth time in a row, consider that Kevin has a beard, a shaved head, and makes a decent salary, and reply:

"Young daddi."

"So, more pics of me with babies?"

"It's more to do with having a grown up lifestyle. I can see your brand coming to its own at a wine tasting weekend, or a cooking class. I'm not saying go to these things. I'm saying that's what you could sell."

"On Tuesday night I shelled peas for the first time and made a pazole."

"There you go. Don't tell me I don't know people."

Then Kevin texts me that we can work on it, that his Instagram is going to be all knees with ice packs and home-made pazoles, I text back, "sexi", and go to bed.

57

On Wednesday morning I wake up around 10am and stay in bed for another hour or so, during which I exchange naked pictures with four different people, living in Hawaii, DC, Houston, and Chicago. I forward the highlights of these exchanges to Peter and Hunter: just a series of mainly faceless body shots taken by muscular gay men in bathrooms, gym locker rooms and bedrooms for private, yet national distribution to other gay men they have never met.

When Peter asks me exactly how many guys I am talking to on a daily basis, I admit that I don't really know and offer to count and come up with a definitive number based on my text messages over the last three days. The rule is that if I have exchanged any flirtatious message, any shirtless or naked picture, or if I have any intention of ever sleeping with this person (or have slept with him before), they count as a romantic prospect. I go through my texts and it turns out that my current number, the number of guys I am talking to, is 27. Peter comments that this sounds like a full time job, and maybe it is, but what else do I have to do?

Following the nationwide picture exchange, my day starts off casually with a coffee date at 3pm. This is with a gentleman I matched on Tinder. His name is Carter. Because neither of us actually likes coffee, this ends up being a walk-on-the-beach date. Carter's strengths are his blond, flowing locks, his superhero jawline, a seemingly ideal balance between bro and prep, his perceived height, and promises of a wholesome lifestyle, full of sunsets and skiing trips and beers on the beach in tropical islands (based on his online profile anyway). Also he seems to be able to form engaging, full sentences very successfully, implying that sometime somewhere, he received a good education. The beach date goes well, Carter is smart and interesting, but he is also eleven years younger than I am, and the couple of times that our arms brush against each other as we walk on the beach my heart does not skip a beat, so I doubt we'll ever see each other again.

At 7pm, I have a second first date for the day with someone from Grindr. This is going to be a gym date. This is a gentleman called Tim, who just moved to LA from Alaska. Tim's strengths are the fact that he's ginger and has some very well formed pecks with really pink nipples. End of list. Tim rocks up at my gym and within the first twenty seconds of meeting each other he's brought up dinner and asked me if I have plans and I'm not a quick enough liar to say that I do, so I guess we're now having dinner together as well. Tim is extremely talkative and loud and he's annoying the hell out of me during the workout, with a choice of such diverse topics as physical fitness ("Everyone asks me what I did to look that way that I do but I don't know, man, it just happened"), career choices and progression (he is currently studying to get a real estate license and working for a moving company where he's helping a lot of "A-List celebs like Chelsea Kane from *Baby Daddy*" move houses while creating unbreakable bonds with them meaning that they will use him to find their next multi-million property when he's a qualified realtor), and international politics (something about Japan and turn of the century Argentina, I don't know).

Worst of all he's the first person I've ever trained with in my gym, so all the straight bros that I see every day and obsess about will now think that he's my friend and, consequently, this is what all my friends are like. I would have preferred to stay known as the mysterious, quiet fag that looks at them thirstily from a distance, with no more information as to who I might be.

After we finish this mentally excruciating workout, Tim asks how we're going to do this, are we driving in one car, are we driving in two cars, are we going straight to the restaurant, what the hell is going on, and I suggest that we stop by at my house first, get changed there and head to the restaurant together. I'm sorry, but I might as well get something out of this, plus his thighs looked pretty good when we were doing leg press. So we drive to my place and shower together and cum in each other's mouths and that's not something I usually go for, but I'm in my mid-30s and quickly running out of all options, so I might as well get off my high horse and deal with some guy blowing his load while I'm sucking his dick and forget about it and move on.

Our shared experiences so far must be enough to convince Tim that we are now boyfriends, so on the way to the restaurant we starts referring to us as "us" and making plans for every day of the rest of the week. At one point, while we're looking for parking, he says that he'll bring his bike over and leave it at my place so we can ride around if I don't want to drive everywhere all the time.

Around 10.30pm I say that I really need to get going because I have to go to bed and get up early in the morning for work. He comments something like, "all right, let's go and get you to bed then". We pay and walk away from the restaurant with him holding my hand. In the lift on the way up to my apartment, where I'm hoping that he's just going to pick up his bag and leave without wanting to make out again, he says:

"It's good that you have to get up early, cause that means I can beat traffic."

I suddenly realise that he thinks he's going to spend the night. I tell him that, I'm sorry, but I don't think this is a very good idea because I really want to take things slowly, and he eventually leaves five full hours after we met.

Today has been really exhausting. I just want to sleep.

Just before midnight I receive a text from someone I spoke to on Grindr months ago and who lives just a few blocks away from me, but we've never met. I don't know what his name is because I never saved it on my phone. He says:

"Thinkin bout u."

I write back:

"Aw."

The rest of the conversation goes like this.

Anonymous neighbour: "Whatcha up to?"

Me: "Getting ready for bed. You?"

Anon: "Just lying in bed right now. Wish I were tucking you in."

Me: "You'll have to do that one of the upcoming nights."

Anon: "I'd like to. Getting pretty impatient lol."

Me: "It's coming."

Anon: "What are we waiting for."

Me: "An evening when we're both free."

Anon: "What are you wearing?"

I take a picture showing my underwear and thighs and send it to him as a response.

Anon: "Ur killin me.."

Me: "You like that?"

Anon: "Yes."

Me: "Good."

Anon: "I'd like it more with the boxers off."

Me: "You wanna see that?"

Anon: "Yes."

Me: "Are you sure."

Anon: "Yes."

Anon: "I'm sure."

I send him a stock picture of my dick.

Anon: "Fuck.."

Anon: "That's hot."

Me: "Thanks."

Anon: "I'd love to see that in person right now."

Me: "Show me something."

Anon: "What do u wanna see."

Me: "Ass."

He sends me a picture of himself lying on his front with his ass sticking up. He looks good.

Me: "Damn boy."

Anon: "Yeah?"

Me: "Aha."

Me: "I wanna see that in person right now."

Anon: "I'd like to show you."

Me: "Why don't you."

Anon: "I will. Are you inviting me over?"

Me: "Ye."

Anon: "What's your address?"

He comes over and I fuck him. He leaves but now I can't sleep. I go on Instagram and see that Hunter is also still awake, because he's just liked a bunch of pictures. I text him:

"I had three dates today. I shook hands with the first one. Exchanged BJs with the second. And effed the third."

Hunter writes back:

"What a 'great' life."

"I know. I'm so proud that my only connections are with people I'll sleep with once and never see again."

Then I take some G and pass out.

OCTOBER 2014

58

Yesterday afternoon I flew in to San Francisco. I'm here visiting with Willa and staying at her house, but also since I'm in a new city, I might as well find some random hook-ups. San Francisco counts as a new city even though I spent three months here last year, because I'm sure all the people I fucked over and the people who fucked over me, have all forgotten about each other and whatever petty grievances we had, and we are now ready to forgive each other and get drunk or high together and fuck. I have Grindr to rely on as always, of course, but I also already have a first candidate and the first candidate is a guy called Cameron who randomly added me on Facebook about three months ago.

Cameron was possibly attractive and seemed to have a nice body, but his profile didn't give too much away, there weren't enough pictures and at the end of the day I wasn't quite sure what he looked like. Then at some point he uploaded one of those videos that people got involved with en masse for three weeks where they took off their clothes and got soaked in ice water to raise awareness for some charity and also their tight bodies, and I was sold. That video fad was very useful, in fact. Because now you could see what people's bodies looked like on video, outside a carefully posed and edited picture, plus you could hear their voices and see if they're masc (or at least if they can fake masc for three sentences, which is fine by me) or if they're just an effeminate gay with a worked out body. So Cameron's ice bucket challenge video was quite good, he wore a robe (which, fine, was a bit fem, but passable), took off the robe, said his lines in a deep, steady voice, had the ice water thrown at him, showed us all how nice his body looks when it's wet, and I suddenly started talking to him and returning his messages. Before that he was all like "what's up, dude", "do you have skype", "are you around tonight" and all that, and I would never respond because I don't like to jerk off on skype because it's stupid.

189

So then I talked to him for a while on Facebook and then we exchanged numbers and started texting, and during those texts we would also send some naked pictures or whatever but then by the end of each exchange he would kinda freak out a little bit and ask me to respect his privacy and delete the conversations because he's not out or something, and he would promise that he also deletes the conversations from his side (like I give a shit who sees my sex talk or a picture of my dick) and I would sometimes be cordial and say, don't worry dude, I'll delete everything, I've got your back, and sometimes I would be dismissive and tell him to stop being such a paranoid closet case and people have better things to do with their time than out some little muscle guy in the outskirts of San Francisco.

As this kept happening and as his infrequent bouts of contact and requests to Skype were often punctuated by mentions of "his roommate being away" and "having the house to himself this weekend", I started getting suspicious, or rather I didn't get suspicious, it suddenly clicked to me. This guy is not a closet case who wants to jerk off on Skype when his straight roommate is away. This guy has a boyfriend that he lives with. It just didn't make sense otherwise. People need to work on better stories. Like, how does a straight roommate stop him from showing his ass on camera to some guy in another city? Why did he have to wait for the straight roommate to be out of town in order to do that? What was he planning to do if we Skyped anyway, get naked, grab his dick with one hand, hold the laptop with the other, and tour the house?

So once I figured that out, the next time he randomly messaged me, which was a couple of weeks ago, the following conversation happened:

Closeted SF guy: "What's good brotha!?"

Me: "All good"

Closeted SF guy: "Nice. I'm heading to Hotlanta today"

Me: "What's happening there? I'm in SF 10-12 October"

Closeted SF guy: "Going for work but hope to have a little fun too. Great news about coming up for an SF visit! Any plans / know where you are staying?"

Me: "Staying with friends and have some plans with them already, but not the whole time. Wanna eff?"

Closeted SF guy: "I'd love to meet ya. Too bad you will not have your own space for a little privacy"

Me: "Oh yeah. That's going to be a problem, I guess. Is your roommate your boyfriend?"

SF guy cheating on his boyfriend: "Yep!"

Me: "I'm good, aren't I?"

SF guy cheating on his boyfriend: "Very"

Anyway, after that he took it to text messaging, because I guess maybe he was worried the boyfriend would get access to his Facebook messages on some home computer or something, and he suggested that we meet up in a hotel room to "have fun" and even though I was still not that interested in the guy, this was now becoming a very complicated, highly dramatic and sleazy affair with emotional stakes and general ridiculousness, so I suddenly got really into it and said yes, let's go to the hotel, let's be really dirty and sordid and immoral, and I asked him to book it and he did, and this got even better because it turned from a hotel to a really cheap, disreputable motel in the centre of the city where people just go to fuck, even though one of the people is a hooker most of the time, you know, the kind of motel that has bright fluorescent lights everywhere, and a soda machine in the car park, and a balcony that surrounds the car park where the doors to all the rooms are, like you see in some indie movies. And the whole sordid affair really turned me on, and this is how I found myself getting out of an Uber and buying a can of Coke from a soda machine in the car park in a cheap motel and waiting for my Facebook date to come back from the convenience store where he's gone to buy a bottle of whisky or whatever it is he's buying in order to mute his conscience and manage to get through this.

I cross the street and walk up to the convenience store where he is. I see him at the till and I wait outside, because I don't want the guy who works there to see us say, "nice to meet you" and hug for the first time, and realise that we don't know each other, but we're about to go fuck in that motel across the street. This is all in my head, of course, and the guy who works there doesn't give a shit, or even if he is bored enough and likes to make up stories about his customers, it doesn't necessarily follow that he would think these two gay guys just met, one of them is already drunk and just bought another bottle of vodka, they are definitely going to the motel across the street to fuck. Wait, now that I've heard it in my head, this is exactly what he would think. There is absolutely no other interpretation of what's happening here from the convenience store employee's vantage point. The question is should I care?

My Facebook date comes out and we hug uneasily. He is definitely drunk and also shorter than I thought. His body is good, lean and tight in a way that photographs well, though I prefer bulkier frames, and I probably should start drinking, as well. We walk back to the motel, crossing the street on a red light because we don't have much to talk about, so we want to hurry up to avoid the awkwardness, and go up the external staircase that leads to the outside balcony where the door to our room is. Once inside, I pour myself a drink from the bottle he's just bought. He's also bought ice, as well as plastic cups, because he didn't feel the glasses provided by the motel were clean enough. He was right. I excuse myself pretty much immediately and take my drink to the bathroom. I check myself in the mirror, undo my trousers, take down my underwear and quickly rinse off my dick in the sink, because, I don't know, I always do that when I know it's about to get sucked or whatever. I pat it dry with one of the face towels provided and do my trousers back up. I notice that he hasn't used any of the towels himself, nor the soap provided, which remains packed in its cheap little piece of motel paper by the sink. Perhaps if he didn't want to touch the glasses, he didn't want to touch anything in the room, I don't know.

I come outside and stand on the opposite side of the bed to him. He's fiddling with a drink by an area he has customised as a little bar, and asks me if I want another. I do. I walk over to him to have my cup refilled and ask whether he's tried putting the TV on. He seems surprised and says no. I say maybe there's a music channel we can put on or something. I find the remote and turn it on and flick through channels, although I don't find one that's playing music videos non-stop because this is not 1997 and he suggests that he plays something using Spotify on his phone. I say, sure. He puts on some DJ podcast or something and asks me if I like it, and I say yes because there is no chance he would ever have randomly chosen something I actually like, so I decide to leave it. The music is very quiet and tinny anyway. We start making out and take each other's clothes off. My initial assessment of his appeal remains. He is sexy enough, but not exactly my type. Which is clearly for the best. As he has a boyfriend. And arranges anonymous hook-ups behind his back. In sleazy motels. And I'm not sure I want to be really into someone like that.

We continue making out and I know already that I don't really want to fuck, but I guess I'm here now, so I go along with it for a while. We are now both naked in bed. After a while he starts sucking me off and he does it so persistently that I'm going to cum. "I'm going to cum if you keep doing that", I say. He stops sucking me off and I ask if he wants to fuck. He's says that he's down to fuck, but then we remember that neither of us has brought condoms or lube. He says, all right, we can cum now, then take a break, go buy some condoms and lube, come back, and fuck. We have all night here, after all. I don't like the sound of any of this, so I say yes. He goes back to sucking me off until I cum. Now I'm completely over it. He says that that was very hot and he can't wait to fuck later. I agree that it will be totally hot and help him jerk off in the meantime. Once he also comes, he says, you know what, I don't think I need to fuck, this was so hot by itself. I thank whatever God exists, lie in bed with him reflecting back on what an incredible hook up we just had for approximately twenty seconds, then I book an Uber to go back home and start getting dressed. By the time I've found all my clothes, the Uber is here, we say goodbye and, once again, that this was totally hot, and I leave.

59

On Friday I am expecting the arrival of Jake Burke, who is a tall, blue-eyed, muscular Denver, Colorado resident in possession of a smartphone and a Facebook account, which means that we have spoken online for weeks, which means that he is now flying over to LA to stay at my place for the weekend. All the preliminary signs that this is going to be awful are there. First of all, Jake Burke is a DJ at a gay bar. Second of all, he exclusively wears high tops. Third of all (although just the first two would be more than enough), a few days ago I had the following conversation with a friend of mine who lives in Denver and knows Jake.

Me: "Hello. Do you know 'Jake Burke'"?

Denver friend: "I do."

Me: "Is he nice?"

Denver friend: "He isn't coming to stay with you. Is he?"

Me: "Yes [frown emoticon]. Is this TERRIBLE?"

Denver friend: "Ummmmmm. He is nice. He is attractive. We have been friends for yrs. He has nothing to say."

Me: "I like him already."

Denver friend: "And he isn't the brightest."

Me: "I see.'

Denver friend: "I have no idea what you will talk about."

Me: "I'll take him to do activities, show him shiny stuff?"

Denver friend: "I do like Jake. But I'm trying to imagine your weekend together and I just can't."

I pick up Jake at the airport and it's 9pm and he's all set and ready to go out to the bars, but I suggest that perhaps since we've never seen each other in real life before, we could probably stay in, have some dinner, say some words to each other, fuck. The disappointment is palpable and it takes a lot of reassurance that yes, we can still get really drunk and high even if we stay in, and then we stay in and get drunk and high, but there is no fucking, because by the end of all the drugs nobody can get it up and I've run out of Cialis.

On Saturday morning, I wake up before 10.30am and find Jake in the kitchen, already mixing up powders from the carry-on bag that he's brought with him (additional to his small suitcase of high tops and clothes) which contains exclusively gym supplements. This is something that he's pointed out to me several times since he arrived, the fact that he needs to check extra luggage for supplements when he travels, so I take it he must quite proud of it. I'm kinda sleepy and want to chill the eff out, but he's pumped up from whatever combination of cracky pre-workouts he has taken and wants us to go to the gym. I ask whether he actually wants to waste part of his LA weekend lifting weights when there's five hundred other things we could be doing, but he informs me that it's only four months until Sydney Mardi Gras 2015, where he's going, and he's really sorry but he's not going to compromise his training schedule now, cutting it so close. (He does not actually say "compromise". I am upwardly paraphrasing). He then shows me an actual countdown of workouts until Sydney Mardi Gras that he has created and keeps on his phone. It's very elaborate and must have taken hours to put together, but at least it provides some insight as to what he does with his downtime between Sundays and Fridays when he's not using his laptop to stream Arianna Grande remixes for the dancing gay crowds of Denver.

We go to the gym and work out separately, partly because we've already started not being able to stand each other, and partly because I don't actually want to work out as I'm getting a weird kickback reaction to his apparent gym obsession. These feelings are very confusing for me and are making me question my whole identity. I expect that if I spent any significant length of time with this person, I would probably just quit the gym altogether. And if I weren't a gym-obsessed, judgmental, insecure gay cliché, who would I be?

On the way home we stop at the grocery store to buy some food and he also buys three bottles of wine. He has finished the first bottle of wine in the time it takes us to go back home, shower, and get ready for the beach. It's always fun for everyone around when people choose to get drunk alone. We walk down to the beach, where at least I get the opportunity to use Jake to enhance my social media profile by posting a picture of him looking stacked and adding the tagline "some boys are bigger than others", paraphrasing the Smiths song, because now everyone will see that I'm hanging out with someone who's bigger than all my exes and that's extremely important for some reason. People will also assume that we're sleeping together, I'm guessing, and the truth of the matter doesn't actually count for anything, because truth doesn't exist and truth is by default what the majority of people believe. Truth is a story. Truth is not a fact. I am sleeping with Jake.

On Saturday evening Jake gets his wish, as we get high as fuck and go out in West Hollywood. Jake chooses to supplement his GHB dosage with a steady intake of alcohol throughout the night, a practice which is very dangerous and can even be lethal, but does contribute to such a high intensity of buzz if you're lucky to stay alive that you might even be fooled to think you are having a good time in a half-empty WeHo gay bar on a mid-October Saturday night. For better or worse we do stay alive and stay out until 3am when Jake decides that he's had enough and we're finally allowed to go home.

On Sunday he wakes up and goes to the gym, but this time I stay at home. When he comes back, I really want to torture him a bit, so I insist that his LA experience must be also a cultural one and we need to go to a museum. It's now 1pm, so he drinks a bottle of wine, puts on some high tops, and we head out. I take him to the Getty Villa in Malibu. We speed-walk through the exhibits for the next twenty minutes as he does his best not to murder me, and I don't know why, but I'm really enjoying this. Once or twice he takes breaks from staring at the floor sulking and glances up to make useful contributions showcasing a very loose grasp of time and space in historical terms, and I don't remember exactly all the things that he says, but I do remember that at some point he tries to argue with me that, in the past, the United States had a monarchy. This conversation goes a little bit like this.

Jake: "I wonder who used to live here in the old days. Probably some king or something."

Me: "I don't think so. You never had a king."

Jake (very subtly unsure of himself but with the forced conviction of an idiot who does not want to back down): "You don't know that."

Me: "I think I do."

This goes on and on for a bit and the only thing that it does is make me miss Lloyd, because it brings back memories of conversations and trying to guess which one is winning at any given point, his drunkenness or stupidity, and I haven't met anyone since then that I can I say I always know the answer for: it is constantly 50/50.

Then we go back home, then we avoid each other for the next few hours, and then I drive him to the airport hoping never to see him again. As soon as I drop him off I text:

"Thanks so much for coming, this was a really fun weekend."

He writes back:

"No thank you for everything. I had a really good time."

And we never speak again.

60

On Saturday afternoon I am scrolling through Facebook and some WeHo guy on malfunctioning steroids has posted a picture from a gay photoshoot he must have done and is really proud of, wearing just white Emporio Armani briefs and holding a very sultry pose. He has uploaded this with the tagline "Sexy Saturday". I take a screenshot and send it to Peter adding: "I beg to differ". Then I go to the gym.

NOVEMBER 2014

61

On Saturday morning I go to the gym, where I'm supposed to work out my shoulders and back, but mainly my shoulders, because they have been a weak point for a very long time and it's getting really embarrassing. I'm doing a set of new exercises that I've never done before and this really stressing me out, making me walk around the gym looking lost, holding an iPhone up that's playing fitness YouTube videos, trying to make sense of it all.

For my first exercise, which somebody somewhere named standing barbell military press, I need a barbell. There's one barbell on an incline bench nearby, so I walk over to it and start picking it up. Then some guy comes back and tells me that he's still using it. Then I stand there again more lost, but now also disappointed. Then I notice that my straight gym crush (one of the Top 25 anyway) who's using a different barbell on a different incline bench right next to me is trying to make cautious eye contact and catch my attention, but in a very tentative way, plus I'm wearing headphones and he can't really talk to me.

This seems like it goes on for an eternity if the feeling in my lower abdomen is anything to go by, but in human time and space terms it's probably only 2-3 seconds before he actually opens his mouth, I remove my left headphone and he asks me to spot him for one last set, and then I can have the barbell if that's what I'm looking for. This is exactly what I'm looking for and a little bit more, so I mumble "sure" and I go stand behind him as he's doing one last set of incline chest press while I breathe in each time he exhales in agony in the general direction of my face.

My straight gym crush is about 6'3" tall, has very short, light brown hair and an outdoor tan, the face of a G.I. Joe action figure but with hesitant eyes, and a tight, muscular, yet lean upper body. He also has really big, strong legs, perhaps more muscular than his upper body, which is pretty much my favourite thing anyone can have, and I assign this to him playing some particular, highly imaginary sport that mainly utilises lower body strength, even though my friend Hunter says that I'm just making this up because I want this guy to be a masc jock who kills it at sports, but it's just probably the way he's built.

For this exercise he was going for six reps, he said, but he only manages five, with my assistance only needed for the last one. We quickly recover from this highly sexual activity (in my head only, but still) by removing the weights from the barbell together.

"How many do you want on?" he asks.

"None of them", I say.

He takes one side and I take the other, and he really doesn't have to do that, so I stutter "thank you" and "thank you so much" an inordinate amount of times, as he goes between the barbell and the weight rack.

Then we're done and I'm about to remove the barbell and take it away and he walks up to me one last time with a face that hasn't shown any expression throughout our interaction apart from physical strain as he was doing his exercise, offers his hand for a fist bump, which I incompetently return, and says:

"Thanks boss"

I die a few deaths inside, and continue with my workout, both ecstatic and also devastated, in the way that you would feel if you knew you had just been touched by the hand of God…via a fist bump…while he called you "boss", but having no way to tell if the experience will ever be repeated, or if that right there was your life peaking and you're now faced with slow, excruciating drudgery until you finally expire thirty or forty years from now.

Hunter and Peter are away for the weekend, so in order to fill the rest of the day, I have arranged to go on two first dates with people I've met online. This is going to be a real stretch in terms of socialising and at this point I have about 0% confidence in myself that I'm going to go through with both, but these are two people I have avoided meeting and even cancelled on already over the last few months, and this month I'm trying to be less of an asshole, so we'll see.

I meet the first date at a shopping mall in Santa Monica. It's 4.30pm.

He doesn't have a plan of what he wants us to do and neither do I, so I suggest that we go to GNC to buy some supplements, because, you know, these are the people we are and these are the things that we do. At GNC I buy a bulking protein powder that has 1,000 calories per serving and you're supposed to take once a day in addition to your regular meals to put on weight, but last time I bought it I found that it was so filling that after I drank this thick, potent chocolate-flavoured sludge, I felt so sick that I couldn't eat for the rest of the day, therefore completely defeating its purpose. Perhaps this time it will work better.

After GNC we walk around and have some ice cream, then walk down to the beach and watch the sunset. I think he and I have enough conversation for just over an hour, but around 5.45pm we're basically just standing there watching the sun sinking into the ocean in complete silence. He checks his phone, I check my phone, he asks me what I'm doing later, I say that I'm meeting some friends for dinner at 8pm and he wonders how much time is left on the meter where he parked. We decide that it's imperative that we go and check to avoid him getting a ticket, even though I distinctly remember that he said he said he paid for three hours when we met at 4.30pm, as it seemed highly ambitious to me even back then.

On the way to the car, he asks me whether I want to walk back home or he can give me a lift, and I take the lift. When we get there and he's about to drop me off, he remembers that he needs to use the bathroom before he drives off, so I offer that he comes upstairs and does just that. He leaves his car on the street double-parked with the hazard lights on. He comes upstairs, uses the bathroom, we tell each other what a nice time we had, move in for an awkward goodbye hug, start making out, go to the bedroom, he tells me that he has something to say to me and hopes it's all right, I say go on, he says that he's HIV positive but undetectable, I say that's fine, thanks for telling me, I wasn't planning on having unprotected sex anyway, and then we fuck.

When this is all done, I want to go on the second date so little that I'm thinking of drowning myself in the bathtub to get out of it. I fill it up and climb in, but I can't bring myself to go through with it, so I suppose this suicide attempt will just have to serve as an actual bath, and I will just have to go on a second first date in the space of four hours.

My second first date picks me up from home at 8.30pm. We drive to Abbot Kinney in Venice to find a place to eat. Clearly I haven't booked anywhere, since only forty-five minutes earlier I was thinking of terminating my own life to avoid being here. My date is a very hyper, self-proclaimed Type-A personality little guy on steroids, talking 6,000 words a minute, living his life on a constant pre-workout high.

We drive past a restaurant we both like the look of. He decides to call them from the car to see if they have any space for us. He connects through the car stereo and talks to the hassled Australian hostess. His opening line is:

"Are you on a wait right now?"

This is very confusing for me, as well as to the unfortunate girl on the other end of the line, who has to decipher his weird choice of jargon through the poor connection of a moving vehicle, plus the loud conversation of the 120 people she's standing in the middle of at a packed restaurant on a Saturday night. Once he rephrases to something more conventional / human, we are able to acquire the information that, yes, they are very busy, of course, but there are some cancelations and they will be able to fit us in. My date then proceeds to enquire whether they have a table in a "nice garden area", despite not knowing what the layout of the restaurant is like at all, although having just driven past and seen that there is no outdoor space might have cleared that up. The hostess laughs in an uncomfortable way that indicates she is now aware she's dealing with a lunatic who has no intention of eating there tonight, and says that, no, unfortunately they don't have a garden area. Not quite done yet, my date then asks if they possibly have a "booth" we can sit in, the hostess says in an icy tone that we'll have to come in and see what's available then, my date says, awesome, see you in a bit, we park the car and go to a different restaurant.

I am back home alone by 11pm eating dinner leftovers that I brought home in a box and watching repeats of Poirot on Netflix.

62

On Saturday this week, we all decide to go down to Laguna Beach and spend the day at Hunter's parents' house. Hunter's parents are away for the weekend. This is part of an overall plan to diversify our activities and not do exclusively things that revolve around the gay bars in West Hollywood and Grindr. After fighting off conflicting ideas from Peter, who wanted us to go to San Diego or Las Vegas and spend the weekend at gay bars there and with a whole new set of Grindr search results, six of us drive down to Orange County on Saturday morning.

Orange County is a lovely, beautiful place that you have to be extremely unfortunate to have been born and brought up in, for no other reason than the fact that, if you're from there, you really have to go out of your way to experience what the rest of the world has to offer. If all you've ever known is eternal sunshine, your parents' swimming pool, and the golf course of the local country club, why pick up a book to read some dead guy's from the last century reflections on the human existence? Why ever move to Copenhagen for a year? If you're born there, you already are where everyone else is trying to get through their life journey, but instead of getting there at 55 after thirty years of hard work and having learnt all your life lessons, you just land in your beautiful, formulaic mansion as an infant.

This Saturday, we celebrate Hunter's Dad's achievements, by spending the whole day swimming in the pool, shooting hoops in the basketball court, and hanging out in the Jacuzzi. I take it as a huge personal achievement that I don't text any sexual prospects for the whole day and don't seek romantic validation from any of the men that I otherwise talk to. If I actually believed that humans can progress, I would think this is growth.

Then it really becomes apparent that, indeed, there is no growth at all, because we all get bored and decide to go back to LA and go out.

There is always the severe danger that if I step out anywhere in Los Angeles on a Saturday night Lloyd will be there and I will see him and my heart will crack in new places where it hadn't cracked before, but at this point I am too drunk and too high for this to be a concern that will stop me.

First we go to some house party up in the hills. The only thing that we know about this house is that it's owned by some exceptionally rich guy from New York, who only comes to LA a couple of times a year and this is not one of them. In the absence of the house owner, the party is hosted by his young, unattractive boyfriend, and the few bits of information that this person decides to share while he's giving us a tour of most of the rooms and all of the servants, are the following: he used to be an actor, he is now still an actor but also working on a few writing projects, the house chef really excelled himself with the dinner he prepared earlier, and the only instruction that was given to the architects who redesigned the house last year when it was purchased, was "there is no budget." I don't know if those people come up with these lines on the spot, or if they practice them alone first and then bring them out in group situations, or…I don't know. It's baffling.

Then I see a guy at the party who's relatively attractive, via having nice biceps and a very full ass anyway, and I believe I'm friends with him on Facebook though I've never met him before because he lives in New York also, so I decide to dedicate the rest of my evening to him. His name is Porter. Porter reveals early on in our interaction that he has a boyfriend back home, but he's also pushing his butt against my crotch whilst making out with another guy when the three of us go into one of bathrooms to share some coke, so the messages that I'm getting here are somewhat conflicting. In any case, this seems like a fun evening and I decide to follow those two out to the bars of West Hollywood when they decide to leave the party.

We walk into the first bar, in practical terms a tiny cube of a room playing annoying 80s disco pop, and immediately bump into Lloyd. He's right by the entrance, standing there with three men that unfortunately the third person in my group happens to know. We all stand in a circle as they say their hellos and I avoid looking in the direction of Lloyd. I'm introduced to the people I don't know by the third guy, and the next time I look around Lloyd has disappeared. He hasn't just walked away, I can see pretty much everyone in this small room; he has actually left the bar. For some reason this really pisses me off. About ten minutes later, Porter and third guy have decided that they really can't stand the music in here, apparently, and want us to leave too. We go out, cross the street and walk into the next bar. Lloyd is here again, this time by himself. He sees me walk in, our eyes meet, he turns his back to me and walks to the bar. I tell Porter that I'll be right back. My state of mind is extremely unsettled and I'm almost hyperventilating. My heartbeat has just about doubled. I push my way through the dancefloor crowd and grab his arm to turn him around at the bar. He pretends that he hadn't seen me before and says hi. For about eight seconds we make small conversation through gritted teeth and then I decide that this is the right time to demand answers to all the questions I've had for him, so I unleash a very angry and aggressive tirade. I ask him why he led me on and pretended to be interested in me when he wasn't. Why he moved into my place when he never wanted to be my boyfriend. Why he told me he loved me. Why he never had sex with me. I ask why he lied to me about everything when I first met him last summer. About his job, about the people he had slept with, about wanting to go out to the gay bars all the time. Why he would freak out and attack people for using Grindr or exchanging naked pics, when it turned out that he was doing the same thing. The number of answers I get is approximately the number that exists inside his head, which equals zero. Or rather, I know the answers, probably better than even he does; I don't know exactly why I'm doing this. Then I decide to focus for a bit on the money that he owes me and refuses to return, which is equally ineffective. Eventually, with no answers and no cash transferred over, we walk away from each other. He walks upstairs to the next floor. I go back and find Porter who's making out with the third guy on the dancefloor. I join them and start making out with Porter as well, who's now dancing between us. Porter grabs my hand and puts it down his underwear, so I proceed to finger him as he takes turns to kiss us both.

Soon after that, we get an Uber to go back to the rich guy's house up in the hills, where my car is parked and Porter is staying for the weekend. I'm under the false impression that for the next hour or so Porter will also be taking turns in getting fucked by the two of us, but when we get to the front gate, Porter says that, despite him wanting me to, I can't come in because the rich guy's boyfriend who showed us around before didn't like me and, he's sorry, but he has a place on the rich guy's dinner party rotation and he's not about to piss him or his boyfriend off and lose it. So I get in my car and drive home by myself.

63

On Monday I wake up at a certain time, which I cannot remember right now, and see that the sun is out and it's really warm, but I'm too lazy to walk the six minutes it would take me to get to the beach, so I go up to the roof of my building and sit there on the deck to sunbathe. I do have a book with me to read, but I'm more preoccupied with texting people on my phone and checking social media. I'm sure that at some point in the future when I am more sexually and emotionally content, I might start reading regularly again.

Today I am mainly focusing on Greg Marconi, who is texting me from Orlando and we've never met, of course, but are Facebook and snapchat friends. Greg has a minor crush on me, it seems, but I am not interested at all because he is a lawyer, has an Italian surname, and has adopted a boastful / hyper-confident flirting technique in order to impress me. Little does he know that he is doing it all wrong and that I exclusively fall for Anglo-Saxon insecure underachievers. Today Greg is telling me the following in order to make me jealous and win my long-distance affection (which, fair enough, is not the highest prize and at least several hundred unfortunate men have enjoyed in the past year alone for a maximum of two weeks).

Greg: "I broke someone's heart last week"

This statement alone is naturally an instant eye-roll, but on top of that I also find it quite unpleasant and unnecessarily cruel, because I have a chip on my shoulder about having my heart broken and I don't think people should be joking about it or showing off. So he's lost me already today. I reply:

"Standard week for Greg Marconi, I imagine"

"You know me too well."

And he continues:

"He was a Facebook celebrity and fell in love after the first time we hung out. I like him but he came on too strong"

"Name?"

"Jack Novak, in real life. Aka Jack Joseph on Facebook."

"Oh. We're friends also. He seems perfectly balanced. I have no idea why it didn't work."

"Everything was ok until he cried when I left to drive home"

"He posts videos of himself flexing, dancing, and singing to the camera ripping off his t-shirt halfway through, boasts about his body with no self-aware nod or self-deprecation and 'complaints' about the multitude of friend requests he receives from strangers. Whilst having a shirtless profile picture and posting all his pictures / videos / updates with no privacy settings, just open globally. This is not a dateable person"

"Yeah but he was man of the day on RealJock once. That's actually how I first knew about him lol…"

"I take it all back"

"In other news, my ex and I have been talking some"

"Interesting. It's all happening around there isn't it"

"Never a dull moment"

Then Greg asks me if I want to go to Pensacola for Memorial Day weekend, then I tell him that Pensacola and the rest of the South is populated by a bunch of drunk, god-fearing, gay-issue ridden 20-year-old idiots, and then the conversation trails off and I am getting sunburnt, so I go back inside.

There, I eat something because it is now lunchtime, get ready for the gym, and text Hunter with:

"I'm getting ready for the gym"

Hunter replies immediately:

"I'm working out at a gym in Culver City because I had a work meeting here. So much sex everywhere"

"Inconspicuous straight bros, right?"

"Yes. There seems to be a subtle league of the hottest ones. They all help spot each other and exchange casual laughs. I want in"

"You may torture yourself for several months…but they will never let you in. Accept it and just observe"

"My youthful, non-jaded spirit refuses to believe this"

"OK then. Just go up to the group and ask them if they think that Riri killed it at the American Music Awards red carpet this weekend like you were texting me last night and see if they welcome you into their group"

Then I don't think Hunter goes up to them and talks to them, and then I go to the gym.

When I come back I go online, because that's where I live, and read comments that members of the Popjustice forum have left about the American Music Awards attendees while I eat my post-lunch.

Reacting to Beyonce's red carpet look, member "TasteMe" has written:

"YAAAAAAAAAAASSSSSSSSSSSSSSSSSSSSS AT HER BODEYYYY!!!!!!!!!!!"

And:

"MURDERRRRRRRRRRRRRRRRRRRRRr MEHHHHHHHHHHHHHHHHHHHHHHH"

"Psychic" has replied:

"Oh. Seems try-hard"

But "TasteMe" is really feeling it and has added:

"Beysus is serving for the GODS and I'm living. That's all that matters"

On Rihanna's red carpet look, "KellyRowlandsWeave" has commented:

"Hmm. Serving me Ashanti 2002 teas"

But "ShadyMatt" really liked it (I think), because he said:

"Rih is giving me bejeweled omelette on a platter"

I read several pages of comments that go like this until the very end, where "TaylorsGrammy" has magnanimously commented, "All the Big Pop Girls brought IT", and then I go out to watch the sunset on the beach.

DECEMBER 2014

64

On Thursday night I'm at home reading the last of *Nausea* once again and listening to *Louder Than Bombs* and this might as well be 1994 and I might as well be a teenager in a suburban bedroom in Berlin, but I'm not, it's twenty years later and I'm in a house in Venice instead and I think those are the only two things that have changed.

At 11.30pm I text Hunter to say that life is very lonely and he writes back to tell me that he had nothing to do this evening and felt very alone and couldn't stay in his room another night. So he went to the park near his house, laid on the grass and a watched a softball game from afar and it was such a nice time. And of course he would like someone to join him, but he enjoyed it. And there's no moral to his story, he says, but yes.

Then Kevin texts me to say goodnight, like he sometimes does, and I inform him of the black hole of self-pity that Hunter and I are indulging in at this moment and Kevin then tells me that this guy he's been sleeping with recently went over to his house tonight to say goodbye before going away for the weekend, they went and got ice cream and the guy told him that he wishes he was dying, because that would be easier than life right now. So I guess Kevin's guy wins.

Then Kevin asks me, "Why are people so sad?"

And the only answer that I have is that, you know what, marriage equality and acceptance all, it's still hard being gay, I'm sorry. We are brought up against the world and we never manage to find peace with ourselves. Kevin doesn't seem that convinced and just writes back "yeah...perhaps" then wishes me goodnight.

Then I text Peter with the screenshot of a guy who friend requested me on Facebook and ask him what he knows about this guy, if anything. Peter writes back that he's a nice guy, he met him while volunteering for some charity project in LA, he has a big butt, huge, but he's too short and ethnic for me.

I write back, "Right. Maybe worth a fuck then", and I go to bed.

65

On Friday morning my next-door neighbour, Elvira, decides to wake me up right before 8am by banging on my front door very loudly. As per usual, I'm inclined to ignore her until she tires and goes away, but I'm awake now, plus this will be my first opportunity to talk to a real-life person this week, so I get up and answer. This is a terrifying thought, but we might be becoming co-dependent.

She bursts into my apartment, takes a seat on the sofa, and launches into the reason why she had to talk to me so urgently. Apparently, our building is being targeted by a gang. I suppose that is a good enough reason.

She was just drinking her morning coffee while staring outside the window, when she noticed a vehicle she did not recognise parked in front of our entrance. Then she noticed its driver (a young man) behaving "oddly but not illegally". He was walking around the vehicle nervously, opening and closing windows and doors and generally pacing in an unusual manner. At one point he reached inside the passenger side window and took something that appeared to be a piece of white chalk. He bent down and appeared to be writing something on the sidewalk. She has now checked this first-hand and there is a short white chalk mark where he was crouching. After doing this, the young man got up suddenly and quickly returned to his vehicle, got into the driver's seat, turned around and drove away. This gave her the chance to note the vehicle model and license number. Elvira then asks me to write this down. I haven't said anything so far, but now I tell her I don't have anything to write with. She says that's fine, but I should memorise it. It was a late model white Ford Expedition with the licence 8HAI550. I tell her that I got it. Then I ask when the gang is coming over.

She tells me that she's not sure exactly what happens next, but she's convinced our building was marked for a hit. These guys are becoming more and more sophisticated, she says. "Yes, they have chalk now", I tell her. She says that's right and what will probably happen is that the gang will come and rob us and then the police will compare the chalk mark with other existing marks in other break-ins and make the connection and solve all the crimes. Then she wants us to go downstairs and take a picture of the mark "to keep on file", but I'm not ready to leave the house at 8.20am, I'm sorry, so I tell her that I have to go back to bed now, but I will definitely go and do that later and the leaves and I go back to bed.

66

On Tuesday late afternoon I'm sitting at home working when I receive a snapchat from Brian. Brian is somebody I know in LA who used to have a boyfriend when I first met him, but now has a different boyfriend because the former boyfriend caught Brian and the new boyfriend in bed together and broke up with him. This story may have a very familiar ring to me, but I'm now on the outside, so I just find it hilarious. Well, not hilarious, but entertaining to hear about anyway, as my heart is not tangled up in it. In any case, Brian was at a chill-out house party I went to a few weeks ago and when everyone was chilling out at the pool, I noticed that he has a very prominent chest that I really wanted to get my hands and mouth on, but he was there with his current boyfriend, plus I was hooking up with the house owner and some other really gigantic guy who was visiting LA for the weekend, and three people is enough, really, anything more than that is just tacky (with very few exceptions, usually motivated by social reasons like we've seen before).

In any case, after that chill-out house party I added Brian on snapchat because I thought he might send the occasional body shot, and here we are and he does. I open this snap and it's him naked and sweaty in front of his bathroom mirror, holding a towel in front of his dick, which makes it very demure and is not crossing any lines at all. Over the picture, he has typed "tirrrrred after Runyon hike". What an opportune moment to take a picture, I think.

The ten seconds that I have to view the picture count down and then I respond just typing a tongue emoji, which I'm hoping indicates I want to lick his sweat off.

I then go back to work for a bit but I'm too distracted now, so I go in my bathroom, take my clothes off and send Brian a snapchat of me naked with my hand obscuring my dick. He opens it and writes back:

"Next time remove the hand".

I wait about an hour and then take a dick shot and snap it to him. He responds with three tongue emojis. I write back to tell him that it's his turn. He writes to me:

"Gimme a minute, driving".

I give him a minute or twenty and then he snaps me a picture of his dick from what looks like a restaurant or bar bathroom. It's all right. I write back:

"When do I get to see it irl?"

He responds with:

"Wht about this weekend"

I say sure and immediately text Hunter, who's in Brian's general friend circle and knows both the ex boyfriend and the new boyfriend and I feel like he needs to know this new development, that Brian is about to cheat on the new boyfriend as well. I'm hoping to get a very dramatic response and create a story, if I'm honest, because I feel like I've stumbled upon something that's very gossip-worthy. Then Hunter tells me that, duh, that's not such a big deal, Brian and his new boyfriend are "open", and then suddenly I'm not very interested in Brian at all, because this is not at all forbidden.

JANUARY 2015

67

On Friday, I wake up at 7am but it's too early and I have nothing to do today anyway, so I take half a tab of Zopiclone, eat a banana and drink a protein shake because I don't know when I will wake up next and I don't want to lose any meals, and I go back to sleep. When I wake up again it's 11.30am.

I check my phone and I have a couple of messages that are from people who are not significant to me right now and a missed call from my Mum and I will call my Mum back, I promise, but first I make a second breakfast and sit and eat whilst checking Facebook.

Jeff Diaz, a very attractive Latino guy who is a personal trainer and an actor or fitness model and dancer that I met at a pool party a few weeks ago and I might have slept with, had I been attracted to Latino guys, has written an update that says:

"Decided on a whim today that I'm going to focus on gaining some weight. I knew I was going to do it, just not sure when. Looks like today is the day due to the fact that I am tired of #GrilledChicken and #SteamedBroccolli and if I have to eat that as another meal, something unpretty might just go down. I now get ot use the next few months changing my diet and enjoying eating the right, flavorful foods that will get me to where I want to be for the time being. Hello #WholeFatMilk #WholeFatCottageCheese #PeanutButter #WeightGainer #QuestBars

Today I'm at 183lbs and the goal is 195/200lbs then I will lean out when I am satisfied. #LeanMuscle I'm hoping it all goes to my butt #Booty #BootyBuilder

#HollywoodLife #InstaFit #MuscleGain #QuestBars #Muscle #Lean #HollywoodBody #CaliforniaLiving #Fitness #ChangeUp"

I screenshot this and send it to Peter.

Gabriel Franklin, an aspiring young actor I went on a date with recently, even though he has a boyfriend, something which I found out later and declined going on a second date with because it pissed me off that he hadn't told me, even though in reality I just wasn't that attracted to him and I used this as an excuse has written an update that says:

"Things I want for my birthday: money, new ray bans, jalapeno margaritas, socks, a pair of dope chubbies, cool Van's, a new car…bmw and above, abs, an even tan, dark chocolate with almonds, wine, money, 55in TV and above..no cheap shit, a brown ass watch, a trip to Hawaii, an iPod, bananas, a pretzel, a reoccurring role on a show…make that lead role, tequila, croutons, a bad ass part with all my friends telling me they all love me. Thx."

I also screenshot this and send it to Peter and add, "You can really tell when someone's grown up dirt poor, can't you" and then I start looking for some porn to jerk off to.

As a first step, I visit a blog that's updated daily with screenshots and reviews of every new porn scene that all the major gay porn studios release. Even though I've come across this blog before, I've never really stayed on it long enough, nor have I paid attention, but I suppose for someone as idle and lonely as I am, it was only a matter of time before going back and getting lost in the vortex that it is, and today the time has come. For the next hour or so, I go through several posts, look at endless pictures of people having sex, and read whole pages of reviews. I identify two or three favourite scenes and then find them online to download for free. I don't want to stream them and get off immediately; I want to delay this as long as possible. As I wait for the huge files to download (because nothing less than HD will do) I go back to the individual blog entries and read the dozens of comments that other socially inept porn addicts have left. This is a new community that I am today becoming a part of, and I think I really like it. People seem to have very strong views about the men that appear in these scenes. People seem to know them, and people seem to have very strong preferences about their appearance, body hair, body transformation over the course of time and between scenes, how they take the d, how they give the d, whether they are gay in real life or gay-for-pay (G4P is a new acronym in my life), whether the flip-flop in the scenes or are strict tops or bottoms, what steroids they should be on, when somebody has taken too many steroids, and how they have advanced from entry-level studios with bad lighting and minimal direction, to more professional ones where they're finally reaching their potential. I'm starting to find this aspect of pornography even more sexually gratifying than watching the sex.

Then my first scene has downloaded, and I watch the entire half-hour clip until the end without touching myself at all. When that's over, I start watching the second scene, which is now also ready. Again, I watch the whole thing, but blow my load in a pair of underwear I've picked out of the laundry basket near the end when all the performers also cum.

It's now around 3.30pm. I go back on the blog and search by name to find more clips from my two favourite porn actors from the two clips I've just watched. I find a couple more clips that I think I will like, and start downloading them. I go back and read the comments that people have left for those, and then watch the third clip that I had previously ignored. I jerk off to this and cum about halfway through.

As I wait for the latest two scenes to download, I realise that I haven't eaten anything for a few hours and take a break from staring at my computer screen to make a snack.

At 4.30pm, I go back and watch the two new clips back-to-back, ejaculating at the end of each one. I have now cum four times in the last five or six hours. The fact that I am now a sad, lonely loser who has spent the whole day jerking off is making me feel disgusted with myself, but is also turning me on. I want to see how far I can take it. I go back and find more videos that I want to watch. I start downloading them, and then step away from the computer again to take a break, during which I read about five pages of *The Tunnel* by Ernesto Sabato, which is my favourite book that I've started reading this year, but I am completely distracted by porn right now, so I go back and start re-watching my recent clips.

By 8pm, I have jerked off another two times. Because I feel worthless and because I am realising that this could easily be the beginning of a serious sociopathic condition, I force myself to get dressed and go to the gym to work out. At the gym I just picture everyone having sex anyway and get really annoyed when neither the receptionist who's relatively hot, nor this blond kid in the weights area who's actually very hot make embarrassing small talk with me, then proceed to take their clothes off and start sucking me off before we all fuck together in the locker room, so I do a half-arsed workout for forty minutes and then go back home. I watch two of the clips again, and cum for a seventh time today.

I follow this up by watching YouTube clips of Joni Mitchell performing *Both Sides Now* first in 1970 and then in 2000 and this makes me really, really fucking sad, like, I don't know, my life is halfway over and I haven't even reached any great epiphanies yet, and then I start texting my friend Anthony to ask him how his trip back to London has been. Instead of texting me back, he FaceTimes me and I'm feeling brave so I answer and we talk for a while, then he brings up this guy that I went on a date with last week, asks me how it was and whether I want to see him again, and I think back, answer that the guy picked me up in a Fiat 500 and, really, there's nowhere to go from that, Anthony agrees, we hang up, and I go to bed where I listen to Björk's *Heirloom* on repeat in my headphones until I fall asleep.

68

On Saturday evening Hunter comes over to hang out in Santa Monica because we haven't spent any time together just the two of us in weeks, plus his boyfriend is away, so I don't think he has anything better to do. First we go down 3rd Street and walk around the shops. I want to buy a basketball jersey to wear at Coachella, plus a flowery headband to also wear at Coachella with the basketball jersey, because I want to have this combined feminine / bro look, which I came up with because I still think of the story of that Greek teenager who got bullied for being effeminate or gay or something along those lines, and then he went missing for a month, and then they found his body. And I still feel a little bit guilty for perpetuating this stupid heteronormative ideal, where all of us have to act like straight bros all the time and nothing else is acceptable, and I think that maybe being a little bit more explicitly feminine at times, wouldn't hurt anyone, and if people have a problem with it, they should come up to me and we can discuss it.

So we go to Urban Outfitters and I buy a vintage Lakers jersey from 1992 or something and then we go to Tilly's and I try on several flowery headbands in the women's accessories section and decide to go with one that sits on top of your head like a crown and has several little daisies on it. When I'm there doing this, two entry-level cute girls in their 20s come up to me and tell me how good it looks, and I know that they don't mean it, and I know they're making fun of me, but I'm also happy this has happened, because this is exactly the kind of low-stake gay bashing that I expect to happen, and maybe eventually some day people will get used to other people wearing all the daisy headbands they want and acting however the hell they like, and nobody will care.

Then Hunter and I get something to eat at Chipotle and then we go home. At home we just sit around for a bit and listen to some music, a mix of 2Pac and Sky Ferreira, but only the pop years, and we watch part of the film *Fools Rush In* with Salma Hayek and Chandler, but certainly not the whole thing. Then Hunter tells me that, by the way, he's staying over to avoid getting stuck in the beach traffic when he comes back the next morning, and I say OK, but also ask if he's brought his toothbrush with him, because he's certainly not going to bed without having brushed his teeth. He says that no, he hasn't, and we walk to the store to buy him one. Also I'm running low on toothpaste. It's after 11.30pm at night.

We walk into the grocery store and head to the aisle where one might find the toothbrushes, but as we walk through I catch glimpse of a masc bro in shorts and a t-shirt and a girlfriend, and I think that he's on a lot of steroids currently, so we take a very brief detour to walk past him. Hunter doesn't see the appeal at first, but then after we've been past him and witnessed the size of his arms close by, he agrees that this was a very right decision, after all.

Then we're suddenly standing in front of the toothbrushes. Apart from the toothbrush for Hunter, I also have this idea that I need to have a number of new, unopened spare toothbrushes in my bathroom anyway, just in case any other guests want to stay over. In all honesty I stole this idea from a porn star that I slept with a couple of times a few months back. There were always new, unopened toothbrushes at his place, and I really appreciated that.

The cheap toothbrushes that I'm interested in bulk-buying come in packages of two. I look at the whole selection they have and toothbrushes are available in blue, purple, and pink. One package has a blue one and a purple one in. This is the masc choice. Another package has a purple one and a pink one in. This is a very feminine choice. The third package available has a blue one and a pink one in. I guess this is a halfway choice. I stop there for a good ten minutes and debate with Hunter which combination of toothbrushes I should purchase. I want to buy four in total. I'm definitely getting the masc choice (blue / purple) but for my other two, I don't know if I should go blue / pink or purple / pink. My concern is that the purple / pink combination might be too feminine for my houseguests and it might put them off. Hunter reminds me that I am now an advocate for feminine gays' rights who wears flowery headbands, and I should therefore stick to my newly found convictions, and buy the feminine toothbrush choice. He makes a very valid point, and I walk to the checkout with one masculine and one feminine toothbrush double pack.

Because it's now nearly midnight, there is only one checkout that's open and there's a queue for it, which comprises everyone who's in the store at this time. This serves me very well, of course, because it also includes the steroid guy from the wrong aisle earlier. On a more focused review of the situation, the steroid guy is not very handsome at all, though his muscles remain large. Instead, there is another straight guy with a girlfriend who's queuing right in front of us and this one is heart-wrenchingly beautiful.

I text Hunter "I'm also in interested in this one" followed by an arrow pointing towards him and then Hunter and I spend the next ten minutes staring at the poor guy and praying that the computer malfunction that has immobilised the whole line of people waiting to pay never gets resolved. This guy has an absurdly handsome square-jawed face with stubble, a nose that looks like it may have been broken once in a sports related accident when he was younger, dark hair, and light blue eyes that are framed by the most distinct hot eyelashes I've ever seen in my life, and you know there's something going on there for real when I feel the need to describe some guy's eyelashes as "hot". He also has an incredible, round, muscular ass that's sticking out in his sweat shorts and an upper body that's never been worked out in his life, which means that his incredible, round, muscular ass just happens to be that way. The girlfriend is a solid 3/10. He must be insane.

Then the checkout starts working again and everyone pays and we all leave and Hunter and I discuss the hot guy from the queue for about half an hour and Hunter is equally dumbfounded by his beauty as I am, and adds that, yes, he's out of this world, and if he were gay and also went to the gym, he would be a completely perfect, unequivocal 10/10 and I remind Hunter that if the guy was gay he might have gone to the gym and worked his upper body and been a 10/10, but on this Saturday night he would probably also be at some bar in West Hollywood getting wasted or at home crying because of some gay drama / break up, instead of buying a tub of Ben & Jerry's ice cream with his loving, ugly girlfriend in a remote grocery store in Venice, so he's probably better off this way and we should leave him alone. Then we go home and watch some more TV and fall asleep.

69

On Friday night Anthony and Peter come over and we're supposed to cook dinner and eat and but nobody has bought any ingredients to cook with, even though we have agreed on a recipe, and we get in a car and drive to the store. When we're in the car I'm checking Instagram and I see this personal trainer guy that I follow in New York or somewhere far away, who has posted a picture of a blender, some fruit and bunch of plastic tubs of bodybuilding supplements and his caption is: "Now this is a motha effin protein shake!! Two scoops of Syntha 6, a cup of plain oatmeal, one banana, a scoop of peanut butter, and Tribulus and L-Glutamine" and added the hashtags #diet #supplements #tribulus #eatright #bigassproteinshake. Now this is a guy that is physically perfect and I obsessed over for a while and maybe I like him a bit less now but I would still drink his bathwater. So on the way to the store I show this to Anthony and Peter and say, you know what, we must get a blender, we must a get blender in order to make big ass protein shakes like that and look like him. And they agree, so we take a detour and go to Target instead, which is at least half an hour's drive from my place, but worth it, I'm sure.

At Target we walk around and get to the blender section and the options are almost overwhelming, ranging from ten bucks to several hundred dollars, and Peter asks me how much I want to spend on this, and I say, I don't know, the lower end of the acceptable range, I just want to be like the Instagram guy to be honest. Then Peter points out to me the exact blender that the Instagram guy has, we do a picture-to-life comparison and it is that, and the blender only costs $20, so I say, OK, I want to be like the Instagram guy, but with enough money where I don't have to sell fitness programmes on Instagram just to be able to afford the cheapest blender, so we look at the next section up, I choose a blender that costs $120, decide that this represents pretty much where I am in life, buy it, and we drive to a Japanese barbecue place in west LA for dinner, because nobody can be bothered to cook anymore.

At the Japanese barbeque place I quickly run this idea that I had by them, the idea being that since I decided that homophobia is rooted in misogyny I kinda want to find a way to go against that. And I want to embrace femininity as much as I possibly can, without changing my actual behaviour or appearance. So I'm considering asking everyone to use the female pronouns when referring to me. People should no longer say, "Konrad looks even more of an idiot than usual in his Instagram picture today", they should say, "…in *her* Instagram picture…" but not even in mockery, just in a straightforward way. Because this, a relatively masculine gay guy going by "she", will somehow make a vague contribution somewhere and combat homophobia. Then Anthony asks me if that's what I do all day, sit at home by myself and come up with all these ludicrous ideas, and I respond that, yes, he knows perfectly well that it is. And tell him that he may find me ridiculous, but I'm just trying to make a difference in the world. Then Anthony offers that maybe if I want to make a difference I should just go down to the soup kitchen and help out with the homeless people there instead of asking everyone to call me "she", which will just about make zero difference to anyone's life. Then Peter also offers his opinion (which I didn't ask for) and he's a little bit more accepting of my groundbreaking idea, he sees where I'm coming from, he says, but perhaps it would have more of an impact if someone really straight, and really masculine (not just on-and-off masculine like me) who's in the public eye would make this call instead. And I say, what, like Russell Crowe? And Peter says, yes, or even that football player that I'm obsessed with who's in my iPhone background picture and who is straight as fuck and plays for the Denver Broncos and is 6'5" and weighs 265lbs and I keep tweeting asking him to love me. And I say that, yes, that exactly who should be doing this, that's a fucking awesome idea. And I promise that as soon as I go home I will tweet him and outline this concept to him and ask him if he wants to be part of a really innovative, socially-aware experiment and help people, young gay kids who are gay and scared to come out because of society's totally unfair pre-conceptions and deeply ingrained discriminatory culture. Although I'm pretty sure that I won't.

On Saturday I have dinner plans with my friend William, who's here in California for the weekend for a work conference. Because of that, I don't feel like I need to make any other plans or see any other people during the day at all. One activity planned is enough. It's not warm enough to go to the beach, so I stay in bed for a good while, get up just before midday, have breakfast, kill some time buying old vinyls of albums I used to like when I was a teenager on Discogs.com which will really depress me when they arrive, because the last time I held these records in my hands I was 15 and I'm sure I had some hopes and dreams and some expectations of how it would all turn out and look at my fucking life now, and then I go to the gym.

When I come back, I get ready to go to this dinner and I even have to make an effort because it's at an expensive restaurant, so I dress like my parents sent me to private school in Switzerland when I was young but they stopped funding me in my early 20s and I haven't reached the age where I'll get access to my trust fund yet, because it's nice to look rich, I'm sure, but if the look is too straightforward and there's no tragedy involved, it's very tacky, I'm sorry, and I leave the house. As I step into my car, I get a call from William and he sounds really sheepish, like he's about to cancel on me and I'll get mad at him, and he cancels on me, but I don't get mad. He and some other guys that he knows here in LA have decided to go down to Palm Springs this weekend instead, there's White Party happening there, and they want to leave tonight instead of tomorrow morning so they get to all the good daytime parties tomorrow nice and early instead of being stuck in traffic. This plan does make sense. He also asks me if I want to go, but I'm really over it and I don't, so I say have fun and go back to my apartment.

Because it's Saturday night 8pm and I have nothing to do and haven't spoken to a real life person today and now I'm actually bored as fuck and want a quick thrill, I message some guy back that I was talking to on Grindr earlier in the day with no intention to meet. This conversation goes like this.

Me: "Hi"

Grindr guy: "What's up"

Me: "So, I'm basically free"

Grindr guy: "Where r u"

Me: "I'm home in Venice. I don't mind driving over there"

Grindr guy: "I'll be home around 10. Is that too late"

Me: "No, that's fine"

Grindr guy: "Ok. I'll text u once I'm about to arrive home"

Me: "Should we find out anything else about each other, like our names, what the favourite band we saw at Coachella was, etc, or are we just going by a couple of pictures and straight into it?"

Grindr guy: "I'm up for anything"

Me: "Kinda like the idea of turning up without knowing your name"

Grindr guy: "Let's do it then"

Me: "aight"

Then I send his pictures form Grindr to five of my friends and ask them if anyone knows who he is and two of them text back and say they have hooked up with him and his name is Alex and he is a dentist and he seems like a bit of an spoilt asshole but has a nice apartment and a nice ass and I won't regret it.

Then I wait around and suddenly it's nearly 10pm and I text him again and this happens.

Me: "Should I set off soon?"

Grindr guy whose name is Alex and I pretend not to know that: "Hey man I'm really sorry but tonight is not going to work. My friend is having a really odd emergency right now so let's get together another time again sorry"

Me: "Ah ok. No problem dude"

Then I go on Grindr for another couple of hours with no effect, and then I go to bed.

On Sunday I get up late again, because this is my life now, and wait for Hunter, Peter, Anthony, Kevin, and Kevin's new boyfriend to come over and pick me up at 2pm. At 3pm, they ring my buzzer and I go down.

We go to the beach and walk around and take some pictures and buy some cheap sunglasses and eat some food and then decide to go check out the Venice Canals, because it seems like a fun, low-key activity, and like I said the weather is not good enough this weekend to hang around on the beach. Also I kinda want to recreate a picture I saw some straight bro post on Instagram where he and a bunch of his friends are sitting on a ledge somewhere and they have their arms over each other's shoulders and they're all casual and shit and it would all be very normal and nice, apart from they have all dropped their pants down to their ankles and are sitting there in their underwear. When I present this idea to the group they're generally up for it, and in fact Kevin recognises this as an actual thing that people do ("dropping trou" he says, that's what it is) and I'm very excited about the dropping trou concept, apart from three out of the six of us are not wearing any underwear because I hadn't warned them before, so I'm not sure we can do it.

Anyway, the Venice Canals idea still stands and we go there and walk around and find a bridge that goes over one of the canals and seems pretty chill, plus it's right next to a house where a shirtless bro is working out in his garage with the door open, so we decide to hang there for a while. And this is a bro who's tall and tan and blond, what a surprise, and is only wearing a pair of board shorts and nothing else, and his ass looks beefy and perfect and his body is toned and athletic, but not with a six pack like a gay guy would have, just the definition and muscle size a normal worked out straight bro would have, and his feet are completely black from walking around barefoot everywhere, and he's standing there with another guy (shirted, not hot) and he's doing press ups and core exercises and pulls ups and I don't know what else he can do to make me fall in love. Their house seems very rudimentary in décor, in fact the house is pretty tiny and doesn't even seem to have that much furniture in it, with a garage right next to it (where they're working out) and two yards: a fenced one in the back and one right next to the canal with a couple of plastic chairs and a plastic table in it, where they must sit and drink beers after they work out, or so I like to think. They also have a husky roaming around and interrupting their workout and they try to fend him off in a casual, playful way and I kinda want to have their life to be honest. Well, the hot one's not the other guy's. Even if they have the same life exactly, I want to have the hot one's life.

Then we're done pretending to chill on the bridge and walk back to the cars and drive off to get some ice cream and on the way to the ice cream I outline my plan to the rest of the group, my plan being:

I will go there on my next day off work in the daytime to whimsically hang out, take a walk on the bridge, maybe ride my bike, check out the scene, bring some treats to their beautiful husky, slowly get acquainted with the neighborhood and eventually ingratiate myself with all the roommates, and this may take weeks or even months, until an opening comes up in the house, someone moves out and I'm asked to move in. Then, one summer, on a warm Sunday afternoon possibly years from now, they can all come and casually hang on that bridge with me and my bud (and roommate [and lover]), Connor, because that is the name I have assigned him. We'll both have really dirty feet and the husky will come play with him and mostly ignore me, but I will be fine with that.

FEBRUARY 2015

70

For the upcoming Valentine's Day weekend, Peter and I have decided to go and stay in Miami, seeing that we're both already on the East Coast, we have nothing better to do back home in LA, and it's not as warm as Miami there anyway. Plus I've never been to Miami. I finish work with my client in New York on Wednesday and plan to catch a flight to Miami early on Thursday morning, and by early on Thursday morning I mean at 12.30pm, but we all know this means that I have to be at the airport at 11am, which means I have to get a cab at 10.15am, which means I have to wake up at 9am to get ready, shower, and eat, and that is early morning. Peter, who's in DC for the week, is planning to meet me late on Friday evening, because he has to wait and catch his flight after work.

Because of this incredibly stressful situation that I find myself in, I decide to take some Xanax for the first time in months just to make sure that I get enough sleep before my flight. I go to bed at midnight and fall asleep pretty much immediately. I wake up around 5.30am to use the bathroom and take some more Xanax because it worked so well the first time. Then I wake up again at 11.30am. I grab my bags, run down to the street and order an Uber and I'm stupid enough to think that I will still make it, but I must be thinking that I'm somebody else, somebody who turns up at the airport late and is still allowed on the flight, somebody who gets free upgrades by being charming with the check-in staff, that sort of thing. But I am not, so I miss my flight and then take the train back, which takes about an hour, and then I have to book myself back into the hotel because the next flight I could get on is for the same time the following morning.

My revised plan is to hang around, do nothing, maybe go to the gym, then start overdosing on Xanax and sleeping pills early, say around 8pm, go to bed around 9pm, which will guarantee that my interrupted sleep cycle will occur earlier, and I'll be up and running by 8am at the latest, guaranteeing that I'll catch my flight. It's foolproof.

I go to the gym around 6pm and do legs, and then this kid that I slept with two days ago here in New York turns up and starts working out his back and looking hot as fuck, not necessarily in that order. As always, and this is my biggest failing as a human being, once a hot guy arrives within my visual range all my other functions are paralysed, my cognitive ability becomes incapacitated and there's only one thought that my stupid, guy brain is able to form in repeat sequence: I want him so bad, I want him so bad, I want him so bad.

The guy walks up to me and we make casual conversation ("I thought you had left by now", "I missed my flight, I'm such an idiot", etc) and I think I manage to get through it without even letting my hyperventilating show. Then I text Hunter to tell him what's happening and complain about the paralysing effect men have on me, then Hunter texts back saying "men=lyfe" and then I continue with my workout.

I'm sat at the leg press and the guy comes and starts using the lat pull-down machine that's diagonally to my left, only two feet away. We are practically facing each other. He raises his arms and starts pulling the bar down and I'm faced with the fine, blond hairs under his arm, which make me sink into my seat and drop my weight. The thing to know about this guy is that he's a trainee lawyer, ten years younger than me, smart, and very attractive. He doesn't need me. I am nothing to him. He can have anyone he wants. I am fully aware of this and I don't begrudge him at all, still I attempt to give it another shot, pick up my phone and text him.

"You are fuckin gorgeous", I type.

He's actually holding his phone as he receives my text, looks up immediately and smiles at me. I get up and walk away in an attempt to make this less awkward.

He waits several minutes and eventually texts back "Likewise x" with a winking face, while we're in completely different parts of the gym, and this is the final indication that he doesn't really want to talk to me any more or meet up again before I go away, but he's polite and kind enough to at least text back and let me down gently. I come to terms that this will be the first time we text each other, but he will forever have my heart. I finish my workout, get changed and leave the gym.

On the way back to the hotel I stop at a restaurant and have dinner on my own. I receive a snapchat from Kevin back in LA showing a bunch of crumpled up tissues with a tagline that says "sniff", take my cue and text him to ask if he's sick.

"Yup – runny nose and cough", he says. "Can't imagine where I picked that up, ha."

"I don't know a final score of how many people you've slept with this week, so I couldn't help you."

"Total = 1. He was sweet enough to share the sniffles."

"How inconsiderate."

"Meh, I'd say it was worth it. How's New York?"

"I missed my flight to Miami, but I'm eating now and had a successful workout, so I'm happy."

"Good – back to bulking?"

"Yes. But I was also sick recently and have lost weight, so I'm not divulging how heavy I am currently."

"Oh come on, how muuuuuuuuuuch?"

"182", I type, and add nine wailing emojis.

"Well that blows. You have plenty of time between now and Coachella, not to worry."

"I suppose that's my real goal, you're right. And my year-end goal is to be 200, which is insane, but we'll see."

"You've been 200 before though, right?"

"No this is the heaviest I've ever been right now. Well, 185 before the sickness."

"Damn, and you want another 15? Someone's greedy."

"I DO. I was 170 this time last year."

"Whaaaa"

"True"

"Impressive though. You'd be a beast at 200."

"I finally want to be someone that matters."

"Yeah get to it will ya? You don't exist if you're under 190."

I tell him that I know, and start taking Xanax. Back in the hotel, I fall asleep by 10pm, wake up in time and catch my flight to Miami.

The first thing I do at JFK airport is check myself in on Facebook to show that I'm traveling to Miami. This has a dual purpose. First of all it adds to the perception that I have this incredible jet-setting lifestyle, where I'm always having fun, always traveling somewhere, and do I even have a job? In fact, chances are that somebody will comment, "Do you ever work", because people love to think on a singular level and only like to do what has been done about sixteen billion times before. It's like when anyone posts a shirtless picture someone will comment, "Do you even own any shirts?" or if the person in the picture has abs, "Eat a sandwich", and they will probably think that such a witticism has never been heard before. The second reason for checking in at the airport is that it says to the people that I'm friends with and I don't know who live in Miami or South Florida anyway that I'm coming and they should be getting ready to sleep with me.

I get to Miami and take a taxi to the apartment that Peter and I have rented. Because I'm in a new city where I've never been before and because there are many people around that I've never met but spoken to on Facebook or Instagram and I promised that I would go and meet, but in fact I'm really too nervous to do that by myself, I stay in the apartment until Peter finally arrives around 8pm. By that point I'm bored out of my mind, plus I'm now starving because I haven't eaten anything all day, not that this was motivation enough to actually leave, wander around, find somewhere that has food, and talk to the middle man who will sell it to me. Also, because the Wi-Fi in the apartment is only working intermittently, I have reached about 75% of the monthly data allowance on my phone, via some really obsessive and very consistent usage of Grindr and Instagram.

Peter arrives and he's full of big plans, as always. We're going to a house party first, but we're also on the guest list for Soho House and, of course, there's an after party for later. The person who has put us on the guestlist for Soho House is somebody that Peter met on Grindr on the cab ride between the airport and the apartment, so that's guaranteed to work out. I don't particularly want to go to all this, so I suggest that we go straight to Soho House and skip the first house party, but the deal is that we have to go and meet the Grindr guy at the house party first and head to Soho House together with him, because the guest list thing might not be valid if we go on our own. This all sounds very complicated and I'm not really in the mood to have sex with anyone just to get into Soho House, but Peter reassures me that if anyone needs to put out it will be him, so we get an Uber and go to some ridiculous mansion on the waterfront somewhere in Miami.

The problem with gay guys who attend house parties at ridiculous mansions on the waterfront in Miami and have Soho House memberships is that they wear nice tucked-in silk shirts, slim-fitting trousers and smart loafers and Tom Ford fragrances and they're unsexy as fuck. I mean, the dumb, masc musc bros I tend to like are really fucked up and a guarantee for unhappiness, but at least they're hot and don't have blow-dried hair and a keen interest in minimalist interior design and low-carb diets.

At the party I don't really talk to anyone and pretend that I'm quiet because I'm really jet-lagged and just flew in from out of town, and when somebody points out to me that New York and Miami are in the same time zone, I explain that I'm European and didn't actually know that, so my jet-lag excuse still counts, and what is jet-lag after all, other than a mental state?

At around 1am we are still there and only now is there talk about moving to Soho House, but there aren't enough drugs and alcohol in South Florida for that to happen for me, so I say goodbye to Peter, order myself an Uber and go back home to go to bed. Before falling asleep I go through Instagram, of course, where, scrolling through the pictures that people I follow have liked, I see a tall, blond, handsome Canadian guy that seems to also be in Miami for the weekend and I want to become acquainted with. I follow him and passive-aggressively like a picture of his from several weeks ago showing some graffiti on a wall back where he lives in Toronto, hoping that he will notice me and follow me back. I choose to like the graffiti picture as opposed to a picture of him (of which there are hundreds) for two reasons: a) to avoid bringing up a picture showing him to my existing followers, so that none of them follow him, and b) so that he doesn't think I'm that into him, immediately giving him the upper hand. Then I fall asleep.

Peter rolls in at some unidentified time and sleeps on the sofa in the living room instead of climbing into bed with me and disturbing me, which is very nice and considerate of him, although to be fair he's so drunk that in the morning I find him passed out there fully dressed without even using a pillow, just face flat down on the sofa, so I think it was a case of stumbling on the first piece of furniture once he walked in and collapsing there.

72

On Saturday morning I wake up at some point before Peter and I let Peter sleep while I check messages and get progressively hungry. The blond Canadian guy that I followed on Instagram hasn't followed me back, which is inexplicable to me, and I can only assume that he's playing some sort of game, but I'm only here for another couple of days and we don't have time for this. I look up his name on Facebook and send him a random friend request. Then I'm so hungry that I'm scared I'm losing weight so I wake up Peter and we go to eat.

During all the eating Peter recounts his evening to me and his stories always sound borderline made up, but that's just because he's very candid and provides great detail and these are all things that happen to most of us, but we don't tend to go back and think of, let alone recount, the sequence of events of our sexual encounters in such minute detail. I'm sure any sex act broken down and recited must seem ridiculous in retrospect. On this occasion, Peter met this person at some club where he went, who was an unattractive, older, short Latino guy, but this guy was really dominant and Peter naturally had no choice but to fall for him. After going upstairs in the club and making out with Peter and making him lick his feet clean, the Latino guy took Peter home, a hotel actually, because he is also visiting Miami, to continue degrading him. This degradation had to be limited to the bathroom, as the friend the Latino guy was traveling with was trying to sleep in the same hotel room and didn't want two random people's sexual role play keeping him up. In the bathroom, the Latino presented Peter with a plastic bag that contained a jockstrap and a pair of knee-high athletic socks (all items in bright yellow) and instructed him to put them on. Once Peter was dressed in this attire and nothing else, the Latino guy requested that Peter falls on the floor and gives him twenty push-ups. When this task was also completed, the Latino guy demanded a dance.

Not a lap dance, an actual dance. Like the Latino was some sort of Middle Eastern king and wanted to be entertained by his harem. With no music on, Peter stood there and danced for a bit in his jock strap and socks until the Latino was satisfied. Then the Latino wanted to fuck, but I think the dance thing has killed it for Peter, who then pretended that he'd taken too much G and was about to pass out and therefore had to leave immediately. Then Peter left.

A Facebook notification pops up on my phone followed by a message. The blond Canadian guy has accepted my friend request and has written to me.

He says:

"We know each other?"

I write back:

"I'm afraid we don't. I just randomly added you." I add a sad face emoji to convey self-awareness of how desperate I am. "I think I saw your instagram.'

He replies:

"Oh, thanks for the add. Where u at?"

"I'm in Miami right now, but I live in LA. And you?"

"I'm from Toronto. But in Miami now aswell."

"Oh that's awesome."

"Went out last night." He includes two dizzy looking emojis.

This indicates to me that he takes drugs. I ask:

"Oh yeah? Was it a good time? I just flew in yesterday and was too tired so I went to bed at 1am."

"It was good. If u have time later tonight to have a drink, let me know!"

"Yeah, definitely I will do. I'd like that."

Then he asks me "whatsapp?" and sends me his number and then I text him on Whatsapp. We make loose arrangements to meet later, even though it's very hard to commit to anything with so many boys around.

Peter and I wonder what we should do for the rest of the day until we have to go to the first party at 7pm. I want to do something cultural that elevates us above all the other gays who go to Miami just to party because we're so clever and wholesome and definitely not like the rest of them, so I suggest that we go check out the Wynwood Art Walk Tour that I found when I was stalking some hot guy's Instagram earlier. Then we realise that this art walk is not in South Beach at all and we'd have to take an Uber for fifteen minutes to get there, so we go to the gay beach instead.

At the gay beach Peter goes and buys four margaritas that come in huge supersize soda-style plastic cups and would be sufficient for at least half a football team post, say, a Superbowl victory, but he keeps them all to himself. I take an MDMA tablet that Peter found in the club the night before. Or I hope that's what it is anyway. As Peter gets progressively drunk and sloppy, he urges us to stand up and walk around the beach, both so that we can see more people and more people can see us. I am really averse to this idea and generally a very private, reserved person, but I end up going.

The situation on the beach is quite dire, with the exception of three people on several courses of steroids that Peter immediately zones in on. One of them is even blond, so I'm also sold. Peter wants us to go walk past them so that they stop us and talk to us and potentially take him home and tag him. I'm actually not feeling very well as a result of that thing that I took that was definitely not MDMA but I still don't know what it was, and follow him there with a fixed stare on the sand / my feet trying to avoid any human contact, even more so than usual. We walk up to them and they do stop us and Peter makes friendly conversation, which turns very friendly, and I don't know how he does it, because within minutes of talking to anyone, whether in person or online, they become dominant tops and they just want to use him and humiliate him. The same people are total bottoms when they talk to other people, of course. I suppose it's like when people talk to me and they figure me out pretty quickly and they just pretend to be super masc and play up they whole bro thing, because that's what they realise that I'm into.

In any case, it's not long before two of these three guys have their hands on the back of Peter's neck and whispering filth into his ear and Peter is lapping it all up and everyone is getting quite hard and

I'm getting quite bored, plus my trip has turned into mild, not really unpleasant, but still not hugely enjoyable catatonia, and I want to go take a nap. Shortly after that we leave, Peter going to some bar with his dom top group and me going home.

Peter comes home in a couple of hours and wakes me up. He is very drunk. I make him drink a lot of water so he can sober up and he gives me some coke and a legitimate MDMA pill, both of which he acquired from his new friends, who finally proved to be useful in some way. He then insists that he gives me a back rub because he says he wants to practice and find new ways to satisfy his tops and I reject this plan immediately on the grounds that it's too sexual between two friends. I have to give myself extra credit for saying no to this even though the MDMA is actually working this time.

We then get ready and go out. I like South Beach. You move from London where everyone has a career and some purpose in life to LA and you think, OK, this is quite different, people don't seem to have a normal office jobs here, but then you come to South Beach and it seems like nobody has ever worked a single day in their lives. It's quite pleasant. Though I couldn't stand the place for longer than three days.

We go to this bar on Ocean Drive and it's quite packed. The incredibly thought-out decoration of balloons, banners, and love hearts around the venue remind me that today is Valentine's Day. I am not emotionally advanced enough for this not to bother me and as an immediate, knee-jerk reaction, I text the Canadian guy from Facebook.

I ask him how he is, if he's coming out, and what he's wearing.

He writes back that he's at his friend's house, which is actually just two blocks from the bar where I am, and sends a picture of himself lying face down on a sofa wearing a pair of green knee-length khaki shorts and white socks. I'm into it. I ask him if he wants to come and say hi and he says that he doesn't feel like going out, he's still tired from the night before, but he'll come and meet me if I like so that we get to see each other in real life.

I get a text twenty minutes later telling me that he's outside the bar. I step outside and see him and I lose my mind, because he's really, really attractive, although I have to admit that I'm really high right now and don't even know what's going on, anyone could have turned up, really. I'm trying to make conversation, but every thought is unfinished and all I know is that I want to leave my friends behind and go home with him. I want to go inside to tell my friends I'm leaving and he says he'd rather wait for me there because he gets way too much attention in gay places and he can't handle it right now, and to be honest I've heard a lot worse from gay men in their 20s, so I don't hold it against him, go inside, say goodbye, and come back out.

He does seem to get a lot of attention from people just as we walk around and this is something very important to me, because I'm an insecure idiot who will never learn. We go to Starbucks; he gets a coffee and I get some water and watch him make flirtatious conversation with the waitress, who is apparently offering to marry him so that he gets a US passport when he tells her he's from Canada. I need to take some sort of therapy that will convince me that being ridiculously good-looking isn't the most important thing there is, even though empirical evidence every day of my life tells me that this is the case.

When we go back home we start taking our clothes off and he pauses for a second and tells me that he really likes me and he's looking for more than sex, I say yeah perfect, me too, and we get naked. Then, as I lay in bed with this handsome, 6'2", muscular, blond Viking from Canada, I start thinking of Lloyd. It's worth remembering that it's been over a year since he moved out of my place and we've had any sort of extended interaction. I say that I need to use the bathroom, grab my phone, go into the next room and check Lloyd's Instagram. He's spending the day on the beach. It actually doesn't matter what he's doing. Any action or inaction gives me the same eviscerating feeling that I can't seem to shake off. I go back in the bedroom, have sex with the Canadian, tell him that he can spend the night if he wants but he'll have to stay on his side of the bed, because I can't sleep with people touching me, take 10mg of Valium and pass out. The next morning when I wake up, I leave the Canadian sleeping in my bed and go outside. Peter hasn't come home and I haven't heard anything from him.

I guess I'll walk around for a bit and find something to eat. I guess I'll then meet up with Peter, maybe go to the gym, go to some party, and find someone new to give my misguided affection to. And then he'll be gone. Like every day in a different place, sometimes in Berlin, sometimes in London, Los Angeles, and now in Miami, I am alone, and the thoughts that form inside my head take over my surroundings. Because everything means too much, and despite the passing of time, nothing ever goes away. And if I were to reflect, try to come up with any sort of life assessment and see what it is that I contributed to the world, the answer would be this: stories about how desirable I tried to be, how beautiful everyone around me was; and how damaged I had become, handing the world back pieces of my broken self.

A LIMEHOUSE BOOKS PUBLICATION

Written by North Morgan
Design by Katrina Clark
Managed by Bobby Nayyar

Typeset in Adobe Caslon Pro and Nevis

© North Morgan, 2016

978-1-907536-81-6

2nd Edition.

Limehouse Books
Flat 30, 58 Glasshouse Fields
London E1W 3AB

northmorgan.com
limehousebooks.co.uk

Printed by Short Run Press Limited. Distributed in the UK and EU by Turnaround.